My Father, Dancing

My Father, Dancing

Stories by
BLISS BROYARD

ALFRED A. KNOPF
NEW YORK
1999

"A Day in the Country" was originally published in *Five Points*. "Mr. Sweetly Indecent"
was originally published in *Ploughshares*. "My Father, Dancing" was originally
published in *Grand Street*. "Snowed In" was originally published in *Open City*.
"Ugliest Faces" was originally published in *New York Stories*.

Grateful acknowledgment is made to the following for permission
to reprint previously published material:
Harvard University Press: Excerpt from poem #754 from *The Poems of
Emily Dickinson,* edited by Thomas H. Johnson (Cambridge, Mass.: The Belknap
Press of Harvard University Press), copyright © 1951, 1955, 1979, 1983 by the
President and Fellows of Harvard College. Reprinted by permission of the
publishers and the Trustees of Amherst College.
A. P. Watt Ltd.: "When You Are Old" from *The Collected Poems* by W. B. Yeats
(Macmillan, an imprint of Simon & Schuster, New York). Reprinted by permission of
A. P. Watt Ltd., London, on behalf of Michael B. Yeats.

Library of Congress Cataloging-in-Publication Data
Broyard, Bliss.
My father, dancing / Bliss Broyard.—1st ed.
p.   cm.
ISBN 0-375-40060-5 (alk. paper)
1. Fathers and daughters Fiction.
2. United States—Social life and customs—20th century Fiction.
I. Title.
PS3552.R79154M9   1999
813'.54—dc21   99-31090
CIP

Manufactured in the United States of America
Published August 2, 1999
Reprinted Twice
Fourth Printing, October 1999

In memory of my father

The greatest poverty is not to live
In a physical world, to feel that one's desire
Is too difficult to tell from despair.

—Wallace Stevens, *Esthétique du Mal*

Contents

My Father, Dancing

My Father, Dancing

MY FATHER and I used to dance together in the kitchen before dinner. I grew up with the kitchen radio always on, tuned to a local R&B station. The habit got started with the dogs; my mother said the music kept them company when we were all away for the day. When I was small enough still to like being picked up, I shimmied in my father's arms while he performed an improvised two-step. Later I squirmed out of his grasp and made up my own steps, ducking out of the way of pots as my mother moved from refrigerator to sink to stove.

When I was old enough to be sneaked into bars—"She's with me," my father would tell the bouncer with a sly grin— we continued dancing to the sounds of stompy live bands. At these bars, dancing was serious business. We sat at a table, a bottle of beer in one hand, the fingers of the other tapping out a rhythm, the bony crack of our thumbs on the edge of the table giving an accent sharp as a cymbal crash. And then we were up, pushing our chairs back, no word exchanged, but both responding to some tightening of rhythm or a deepening in the bass line. That moment reminded me of the way our dogs on the beach would suddenly begin to run down the sand at a breakneck clip, running toward something that seemed to be attached by an invisible string to a part of them not yet bred out.

I relied on this silent method we had of communicating, so I didn't know how to talk to my father when he was lying in a hospital bed, slowly dying of cancer. I hung over him, like an insect caught in a spider's web, thrashing uselessly. I watched for the tiniest movement, a gesture, a raising of his eyebrows, anything that would tell me about what I meant to him.

On those dance floors over the years, we told each other more about ourselves than in any conversation. I mimicked my father's movements, and when I had gotten it right, I felt suddenly that I had been dropped into his body for a moment and knew his pleasure at pushing out on the floor a rhythm that brought the music inside of him. I used these occasions to test him, too. As my body grew and pushed out in new places, I wriggled these parts and tried on different movements, the way I would try on new clothes. He was my first male audience, and I used him as a mirror to understand what I looked like to the world. His eyes told me what worked and what was too much, until I settled into a rhythm that suited me. It seemed natural that I should learn these lessons from him. Once my father told me that he wanted to be the first man to break my heart, because then he could ensure that at least it would be done gently. I thought about this during one of the many hours I spent sitting next to his hospital bed holding his hand. As I waited for some sign that he was aware of me, I thought it had boiled down to this: all I wanted from him was a simple squeeze of his fingers. As I waited and did not receive any sign, I realized that he was breaking my heart and it wasn't gentle at all.

My mother would watch our dancing at these bars from

the table. Usually a woman friend would have joined her, and they would talk, their mouths lifted to each other's ears, hands cupped to their faces like they were telling secrets. My mother liked to dance, too, and at times, when I was younger, I wondered if she was jealous. But now I could see that she must have liked to watch us, her husband and the daughter they had made, proving out there on the dance floor the success of their lives together.

SOMETIMES in the hospital my father and I talked. Or, rather, he talked. He told stories about when he was young, women he dated before he met my mother, friends he had who were, I knew, now dead. As he spoke, he stared slightly below and to the left of the television set. Once I moved behind him so I could match my line of sight with his. Maybe, I thought, the sunlight coming in from the large windows was catching this patch of white wall and giving it a suggestive sheen. But it just looked blank to me. It seemed he was seeing his life projected onto this wall and was giving it voice. I listened for my name and, when I didn't hear it, told myself that he just hadn't gotten to me yet. Once in a while he turned toward me and asked if it was time to go yet. I misunderstood the first time and tried to reassure him with what would become my mother's and my refrain, "I'm right here. I love you."

"Oh, stop with your bromides!" he answered. "I'm a busy man. Get the car and let's go. Let's go! Let's go!"

I quickly learned to lie and would say that we were leaving any minute. He would forget after a while or go back to telling stories about his life.

ONE DAY, while I was riding the bus to the hospital, a blind man sat in the seat across from me. I noticed him at first because of his sunglasses, which were French and very expensive, and which I had coveted in a shop earlier in the summer. Then I noticed his stick and wondered if someone had helped him pick out the glasses. As we rode, he rubbed his foot up against the pole separating his seat from the seats next to him and also stroked it furtively with the back of his hand, from knee to shoulder height. The other riders stared out the window or read or focused blankly on the space in front of them. It struck me that the blind man was trying to make sense of the world around him. As I watched him, I thought about sitting with my father in the hospital, about how I continued to bump up against the fact of him lying there, through my conversations with the nurses about his temperature, his platelet count, and how the night had gone, through the hospital food that we ordered for him, though he couldn't eat it, and which I ate. When his friends came to visit, I waited for them to turn back from the window as they wiped the tears from their eyes. I struggled to see the shape of what would happen as it loomed, invisible, in front of me.

Sometimes I saw things too clearly. One day my mother and I were helping my father roll onto his side so that the nurse could rub lotion on his behind, where the bedsores were worst. I held his thigh firmly in my grip to keep him in place. His lower body had become bloated with fluid. My mother cradled his shoulders in a hug to keep him on his side and said, "Come on, honey. Hug me back. That's it." When I removed my hands, their imprint remained, each finger clearly outlined. My hands are large like my father's. He once said we were descended from road workers and our palms were made to crush rocks. The sight of my mark on him shocked me out of the inertia into which fear had pushed me in the recent days. I looked at the mark again and glanced at my mother and the nurse, guiltily, lest they had seen what I had done. I rubbed my father's thigh, trying to erase my finger marks. This was not the impression I wanted to make.

After my mother and the nurse left the room, I sat on the edge of my father's bed and held his hand between mine, so that my hands were flat and covered his completely, front and back. His hands didn't seem so large anymore. The skin had the softness that babies and old people share. I thought, Here is something useful I can do. I can protect this hand. I talked of things we would do when he got out of the hospital. How we would dance together again. I told him that I had discovered a new band for us called Tower of Power. They had a terrific horn section and good conga drumming too. Maybe tomorrow, after he had rested, I would play the tape and we could crank up the bed. He could dance, I told him, the way we danced in the car during long trips, just moving his shoulders and clapping out rhythms.

When I walked into his room the next morning, my father asked me to come to his bedside. He hadn't said anything to me directly in days. He pointed toward the closet and whispered, "My pants."

I pulled down a pair of sweatpants that were folded on the top shelf. "Here they are, Dad. They're right here," I said. I shook them out and handed them to him.

Then I took the tape out of my pocket and put it on the player, the volume turned low. "This is the band I told you about yesterday," I said. "They're called Tower of Power." I pulled the folding chair out from the corner, opened it, and placed it close to his bedside. I tapped my palms in time to the music on the top of his blanket. My father stared down at the sweatpants in his lap. I turned up the volume a little more. He turned the pants slowly in his hands, pushed his fingers through the cuff of one leg, and looked up at me.

"You want to put them on?" I asked.

"Yes. Yes," he said. His voice was hoarse with annoyance, as if I'd asked an unreasonable question.

"Dad, I don't think that would be a good idea. You have all these tubes down there." He pushed the sheet covering him down to his belly. I tried to pull it back up. "I don't think I could get them over the tubes."

"Get some money from Mommy." His voice was low and hard to hear over the tape player. I craned my neck forward so our faces were very close, and smelled the heady staleness that had become my father's scent. Each time I smelled it, the truth of his lying there flashed through me like a painful forgotten memory. "Get twenty dollars," he said, "and give it to one of the attendants to go buy some nail clippers. Harry would do it. You know, the little guy with the mustache."

"Nail clippers? You want to cut your nails?" I saw that they had gone unattended.

"No, no. Why can't you listen?" He clenched his jaw and spoke through his teeth in a harsh whisper. "To cut the tubes. You can cut the tubes with nail scissors."

I tried to explain that I couldn't cut the tubes, that he needed to stay there until he was stronger. My voice had a whining hysteria to it as I hid my fear behind the cover of an urgent rationality.

"No, Kate. I need to go home." Morphine had made his pupils very large. He looked as if he were trying to stay awake.

The rails on the hospital bed were raised. I stood up to rest my hands on either side and lean over him. I told him that I knew he wanted to go home and added that he would go home soon, but he had to stay here for now and get better. "Dad, don't you want to get better?" The panic I had been trying to hide crept into my voice then and filled the white room. There was nothing in the room to absorb it: no colorful rug, no family photos on the wall. The knickknacks my mother was always discovering at flea markets were not covering these tables. There was only a naked cleanliness and order. Everything was white, and the machines around his bedside were ticking in an urgent steady tempo. I looked out into the hallway for someone to interrupt this moment. My father stared up at me, his expression shamelessly pleading, like that of a junkie. I have always had trouble telling people no, and I realized that my father knew this and that was why I had been singled out to take him home.

"I can't, Dad," I said again, as much for myself as for him.

One of his hands rested on the bed rail next to the folding chair where I'd been sitting. He now gripped the rail with both hands and tried to pull himself to a sitting position. He placed one hand over the other and rose toward me. His head hung back loosely from his neck. As he pulled harder, his torso began to twist toward one side of the bed. Under his arm's lean covering of fat and skin, I could see the stringy fibers of his muscles stretching. "Dad!" I said, not being able to stand it anymore. I rushed for the button to elevate the head of his bed. The handrails slipped through his fingers. He sank back and the rising mattress caught him.

He looked at me and reached out, swatting the empty air as if trying to bat away some invisible adversary. His hand settled on my shoulder, and I was surprised by the strength in his fingers as he pulled me toward him, bringing my ear to his mouth. I was conscious of keeping my face relaxed as his scent pressed in on me again.

"Please!" he said, and there was nothing I could do for him. I drew my head back and lifted his hand from my shoulder. His arm hung suspended between us for a moment. His watch, the strap secured on the tightest hole, slid down toward his elbow. Finally his hand dropped to his side.

The cassette was still going, and the saxophonist played a

bluesy solo. It was the kind of thing my father liked. The intensity of the music heightened. The sax player blew slow high notes. I got up from my father's bedside, walked across the room, and looked out the window. I placed my hands on the sill and rocked my weight gently from foot to foot.

SOON AFTER my father was diagnosed, we went together to the movies in Harvard Square. We were early and he took me to one of the small parks in the Square to show me a band he had discovered. The band was made up of two guys on drum kits, another on rhythm sticks, and a fourth who played two conga drums. The musicians stacked rhythm over rhythm surrounding a collaborative beat. One drummer stood apart from the others. With his head down and his long brown hair curtaining his face, he took his tempo from half time to double time and then back again. His arm hung in the air for a moment and then struck down on the drum skin as he provided his accent to the general beat. My father and I had looked at each other and smiled because we both understood this musician's sophisticated intentions.

I stood back from the windowsill and closed my eyes. I swung my arms in half circles around my body, letting them knock into my hips before they reversed direction again. My movements in this room so far had been small and apologetic. My father's lying motionless in bed made me walk, literally, on tiptoe. He was changing slowly before my eyes, but my body had been tensed as if something was going to happen at any minute. I took a deep breath and let it out through my lips in a noisy hiss. I wanted to take us back to that park.

With my eyes still closed, I rocked my hips back and forth, and the ticking of the machines around my father's bedside blended into the rhythm of the music. We were standing on a patch of grass, and the band was lit by some lanterns hanging low in the maple trees around us. Our drummer saw us and waved one drumstick. We started to dance.

My father took up the drummer's alternative, while I started with the universal beat. He liked to begin with the complex rhythm, to pay tribute to intelligence, to make it known that the drummer was heard. Younger and less experienced, I tarried in the solid underlying rhythm and was content to let my father accent me. He shuffled to the double time and showed the drummer that he had some tricks too. He sang "Ooh! Ooh!" through the purse of his lips. His right leg was thrust out in front of the left and he shifted his torso forward, with a jaunty lift of his hip.

"Come on," he said to me. "Try it for a minute. You can always go back." At first I faltered, following the rhythm too closely. My tongue was pressed against the corner of my mouth in concentration. My father laughed at me and, in imitation, furrowed his brow. "Kate, you're trying too hard," he said. I'll show you, I thought, and lightened my step, and left him behind. I lingered and loafed in the hollows between the beats. I skittered along the edge of the melody, swaggering from note to note. "Yes," I heard faintly. "Yes."

The tempo increased, and I began to spin around. Using my right foot to propel me, I turned faster and faster on my left leg. I opened my eyes briefly, and the flowers lining the hospital room and the machinery crowding my father's bedside dissolved into the scene. There was a garden in the small park, and the machines became tall bushes, their tubes stretching out into thin, fragile branches.

I closed my eyes again. As I turned faster and faster, the sight of my father hunched over, watching me, grew blurred, and the clapping of his hands became a sustained clatter. Other people began to surround me. They yelled "Do it! All right!" Then I was in a place alone with the music. My feet didn't feel the ground. I knew the music was going to stop before it actually did. I stopped, too, catching myself all at once with my right leg exactly on the beat.

I opened my eyes, and as when you wake up from a vivid dream and still expect to be in its setting, I was surprised and disappointed by my surroundings. I was still in the hospital room. My father lay cranked up in the bed, his eyes fixed on the blank wall. The door to the hallway was open. A nurse walked by, and an orderly wheeling a cart of food came in and out of view. I so expected to see an audience in the doorway, wide-eyed and shocked that I had been dancing in my father's hospital room, that for a moment I doubted I had been moving at all.

I sat back down in the folding chair and, out of breath from spinning, leaned forward, resting my forearms on my knees. I moved forward a little more so I was in my father's view. "Dad!" I called out. "Guess what, Dad?" I waited for a gesture, a focusing of his eyes, for his eyes to close. In the park, he had clapped out staccato rhythms. I clapped in front of his face. He closed his eyes. I leaned back in my chair.

My mother walked into the hospital room. She put down her purse and hung up her coat on the hook on the back of the closet door. She looked at me expectantly. I hadn't said anything yet and my silence made her come to my side and take my hands.

"What is it, honey? Is there news? Did the doctor come by?"

She bit down on her lower lip to hold in the rest of her words while she waited for me to speak. Half-formed sentences clamored in my head: about my father wanting to leave, Harvard Square, dancing, all those dance floors. I wanted to tell her how at one time I knew what it felt like to be him, and now I couldn't even stand to look into his eyes, because it seemed that what he saw was none of us but his own death staring back at him. I took a breath and started to cry.

"What is it?" my mother asked again, her fingers tightening around my hands.

"I've been here all along," I said, "but I don't know where he's gone to."

Her grip loosened, and she let her head fall forward. After a moment, she patted and stroked the back of my hand. "I know," she said. "I know."

A few months later, when I walked into my parents' house, the air smelled slightly sweet. It reminded me of the smell when my father had come in from playing football on the beach or when we sat around in the kitchen having a beer together after a night out dancing. I heard some movement in the dining room. My mother was out for the day visiting an old friend in New Hampshire. I called out, "Hello." Our Labrador retriever, George, appeared around the corner with her bowl in her mouth. She looked up at me and thumped her tail against the doorway. I could faintly hear music, a drum and someone singing, but I couldn't make out the words. My mother must have left the radio on for the dogs.

I walked into the dining room and noticed the Revolutionary War rifle hanging over the mantel.

"Gift from an old friend." I heard my father's voice. I turned around the room looking for him. "Talked him out of killing himself."

"Dad?"

"Antique dealer now."

"Are you here?" I walked into the living room.

"This rug." His voice came from far away. I looked down to the rug under my feet.

"Saw it at a yard sale . . . when we were first married."

I knelt down to touch the rug.

"It had just started to rain."

"Dad?"

"Felt we had to save it."

I'd always loved this rug with its border of cabbage roses. When I was little, I would stand on my father's feet and he would dance at my command. "Hop to that flower, Daddy," I would say, pointing to a rose in the opposite corner. He would jump to the designated flower, and I would press against him, wildly laughing. "Now that flower, Daddy," and he would leap again. "Faster, faster," I'd say, and we would leap from rose to rose as I clung to him, never wanting to let go.

I stood up and walked to the bookcase in the corner of the room where the stereo was kept. After leafing through some of the albums stacked next to it, I picked out an Afro-Cuban record of my father's, by Tito Puente, and put it on. I turned the volume up loud. The music began with a conga drum beating the air and a woman's voice blaring out. The singer did not sing words. I listened to the voice expand and contract and could hear the singer experiment with the feeling of the sounds moving around in her mouth, the rush of air through her throat. I heard her breath force through the small space of a kiss. I turned back to the center of the room, and there was my father dancing on the rug of overblown roses, his arms clasped tightly to his chest.

Mr. Sweetly Indecent

I MEET my father in a restaurant. He knows why I have asked to meet him, but he swaggers in anyway. It's a place near his office and he hands out *hellos* all around as he makes his way over to my table. "My daughter," he explains to the men who have begun to grin, and he can't resist a wink just to keep them guessing. "Daddy," I say; his arms are around me. He squeezes a beat too long and I'm afraid I might cry. He kisses me on both cheeks, my forehead and chin. "Saying my prayers," he has called these kisses ever since he used to tuck me into bed each night. They started as a joke on my mother, who is French and a practicing Catholic. Because my mother always kept her relationship with God to herself, the only prayer I know is one my father taught me:

Now I lay me down to sleep. I pray the Lord my soul to keep.
If I should cry before I wake, I pray the Lord a cake to bake.

I only realized years later that he had changed the words of the real prayer so I wouldn't be scared by it.

My father orders a bottle of expensive red wine. He's had

this wine here before. When it arrives, he insists that I taste it. He tells the waiter that I'm a connoisseur of wines. The truth is that I worked one summer as a hostess in a French restaurant where I attended some wine-tasting classes. We learned that a wine must be tasted even if it's from a well-known vineyard and made in a good year because there could be some bad bottles. I could never tell the good wines from the bad ones, but I picked up some of the vocabulary.

I make a big fuss, sniffing the cork, sloshing the wine around in my mouth. "Fruity. Ripe," I say.

The waiter and my father smile at my approval. I smack my lips after the waiter leaves. "But no staying power. Immature, overall."

My father gets a sour look on his face. He's taken a big sip so that his cheeks are puffed out with the liquid. After he gulps it down he says, "It's fine." And then he adds, "You know, it's all right for you to like it. It cost forty dollars."

"I'll drink it but I don't really like it."

He looks ready to argue with me and then thinks better of it, glancing instead around the restaurant to see if anyone else he knows has come in.

We don't say anything for a bit. I'm hesitating. I sip the wine, survey the room myself. I've recently begun to realize that my father's life exists outside the one in which I have a place. Rather than viewing this outside life as an extension of the part that I know, I choose to see it instead as a distant land. Some of its inhabitants are here. Mostly men, they chuckle over martini glasses; one raises his eyebrow. They all look as if they have learned something that I have yet to discover.

Finally, I put my glass down and smooth some wrinkles in the tablecloth. "Dad, what are we going to do?" I ask without looking up.

He takes my hand. "We don't need to do anything. We

should just put it behind us. We can pretend that it didn't even happen if that's what you want."

"That's what you want," I say. I'd caught him, after all, kissing a woman on the street outside his apartment.

As LONG as I can remember, my father has kept an apartment in this city where he works and I now live. In his profession, he needs to stay in touch, he has always said. That has meant spending every Monday night in the city having dinner with his associates. Occasionally, it had occurred to me that his apartment might be used for reasons other than a place to sleep after late business dinners. Then one night, while I still lived at home, my mother confided that a friend of my father's contributed one hundred dollars a month toward the rent to use it once in a while. I remember that my mother and I were eating cheese fondue for dinner. On those nights my father was away, my mother made special meals that he didn't like. She ripped off a piece of French bread from the loaf we were sharing and dipped it in the gooey mixture. "This friend brings his mistress there," she explained. "I hate that your father must be the one to supply him with a place to carry out his affair." I didn't say anything, my suspicion relieved by this sudden confidence. My mother tilted back her head and dropped the coated bread into her open mouth. When she finished chewing, she closed the subject. "His wife should know what her husband is up to. I'm going to tell her one day."

When I was walking down my father's street early last Tuesday morning, it didn't even occur to me that my father would be at his apartment. I was on my way to the subway after leaving the apartment of a man with whom I had just spent the night. This man is a friend of a man at work with whom I have also spent the night. The man at work, call him

Jack, is my friend now—he said that working together made things too complicated—and we sometimes go out for a drink at the end of the day. We bumped into his friend at the bar near our office. The friend asked me to dinner and then asked me to come up to his apartment for a drink and then asked if he could make love to me. After each question, I paused before answering, suspicious because of the directness of his invitations, and then when he looked away as if it didn't really matter, I realized that, in fact, I had been waiting for these questions all night, and I would say yes.

When we walked into this man's living room, he flicked a row of switches at the entrance, turning on all the lights. He brought me a glass of wine and then excused himself to use the bathroom. I strolled over to the large picture window to admire the view. Looking out from the bright room, it was hard to make out anything on the street. The only movement was darting points of light. "It's like another world up here," I murmured under my breath. I heard the toilet flush and waited at the window. I was thinking how he could walk up behind me and drape his arm over my shoulder and say something about what he has seen out this window, and then he could take my chin and turn it toward him and we could kiss. When I didn't hear any movement behind me, I turned around. He was standing at the entrance of the room. "I'd like to make love to you," he said. "Would that be all right?" There was no music or TV, and it was so silent that I was afraid to speak. I smiled, took a sip of wine. He shifted his gaze from my face to the window behind me. I glanced out the window too, then put my glass down on the sill and nodded yes. "Why don't you take off your coat," he said. I slipped my trench coat off my shoulders and held it in front of me. He pointed to a chair in front of the window and I draped the coat over its back. Then he asked me to take off the rest of my clothes.

Once I was naked, he just stood there staring at me. I wondered if he could see from where he was standing that I needed a bikini wax. I wanted to kiss him, we hadn't even kissed yet, and I took a small step forward and then stopped, one foot slightly in front of the other, unsteady, uncertain what to do next. "Beautiful," he finally whispered. And then he kept whispering *beautiful, beautiful, beautiful. . . .*

I had just reached my father's block, though lost in my thoughts I didn't realize it, when from across the street, I heard a woman's voice. "Zachary!" the voice called out, the stress on the last syllable, the word rising in mock annoyance, the way my mother said my father's name when he teased her. All other times, she called him, as everyone else did, just Zach. I looked up and there was my father pushing a woman up against the side of a building. His building, I realized.

My father's face was buried in her neck, and she was laughing. I recognized from her reaction that he was giving her the ticklish kind of blowing kisses that I hated. I had stopped walking and was staring at them. I caught the woman's eye briefly, and then she looked away and whispered something in my father's ear. His head jerked up and whipped around. I looked down quickly and started walking away, as if I had been caught doing something wrong. If my father had run after me and asked what I was doing in this neighborhood so early in the morning, I wouldn't have known what to tell him. I glanced back, and the woman was walking down the street the other way, and my father was standing at the entrance of his building. He was watching the woman. She was rather dressed up for so early in the morning, wearing a short black skirt, stockings, and high heels. She pulled her long blond hair out from the collar of her jacket and shook it down her back. Her gait looked slightly self-conscious, the way a woman's does when she knows she is being watched. Before I looked away, my father glanced in my direction. I avoided meeting his eyes and shook my head, a gesture I hoped he could appreciate from his distance. As I hurried to the subway, the only thought I had was fleeting: My man had not gotten up from bed to walk me out the door.

FOR THE NEXT few days I waited for the phone to ring. Neither man called. I asked Jack, the man at work, if he had heard from his friend. "Sorry, not a peep," he said. He patted me on the knee and said that he was sure his friend enjoyed the time we spent together and that I would probably hear from him soon.

It was unusually warm that day, and I walked home rather than taking the subway. All the way home, I kept picturing myself back in the man's apartment. I saw us as someone would have if they had been floating nine stories high above the busy avenue that night and had picked out the man's lighted window to peer into: a young woman, naked, moving slowly across a room to kiss the mouth of her clothed lover. It seemed that the moment was still continuing, encapsulated eternally in that bright box of space.

When I walked in the door that afternoon, my phone was ringing. I rushed to answer it before the machine picked it up. It was my mother. She had already left a message on my machine earlier in the week to call her about making plans to go home the following weekend. Whether I should tell her about my father was a question that had been gathering momentum behind me all week. My mother is a passionate, serious woman. My father met her when she was performing modern dance in a club in West Berlin. The act before her was two girls singing popular American show tunes and after her, for the finale, there was a topless dancer. She didn't last there for very long. My father liked to describe how the audience of German men would look up at her with bemused faces. Her seriousness didn't translate, he would say, and the Germans would be left wondering if her modern dancing was another French joke that they didn't get. After the shows, all the women who worked there had to *faire la salle*, which meant dance with the male customers. At this point in the story I would ask questions, hoping that a bit of scandal in my mother's past would be revealed, or that at least I would find out that she had to resist some indecent propositions at one time. But my mother always jumped in to say that she had learned that if you don't invite that kind of behavior, then you won't receive it. Such things never happen by accident. My father married my mother, he would explain, because she was one of the last women left who could really believe in marriage. He said she had enough belief for the both of them. I hadn't called my mother back.

"Oh, sweetie. I'm glad I caught you," she said. "You're still going to take the 9:05 train Saturday morning, right?"

"Uh-huh."

"OK. Daddy will have to pick you up after he drops me off at the hairdresser's. I'm trying to schedule an appointment to get a perm."

"Ahh."

"I feel like it's been forever since I've seen you. Daddy and I were just saying last night how we still can't get used to you not being around all the time."

I tried to picture myself back in my parents' house. I couldn't place myself there again. I couldn't remember where in the house we spent our time, where we talked to each other: around the dining room table, on the couch in the den, in the hallways; I couldn't remember what we talked about.

"Is everything OK, honey? You sound tired."

"Hmmm."

"All right. I can take a hint. I'll let you go."

After we hung up, I said to my empty apartment, "I caught Daddy with another woman." Once these words were out of my mouth, I couldn't get away from them. I went out for a drink.

WHEN I WOKE up the next morning, I decided to cut off all of my hair. I have brown curly hair like my father's. It's quite long, and when I stood in that man's living room I pulled it in front of my shoulders so that it covered my breasts. The man liked that, he told me afterward as he held me in his bed. He said that I had looked sweetly indecent. I lost my nerve in the hairdresser's chair and walked out with bangs instead. In the afternoon, I went to a psychic fair with a friend, and a fortune-teller told me that she saw a man betraying me. "Tell me something I don't know," I said, but that would have cost another ten dollars.

I called my father Sunday morning at home. I knew when he answered the phone that he had gotten up from the breakfast table, leaving behind a stack of Sunday papers and my mother sipping coffee.

"We have to talk before I come home next weekend."

"OK. Where would you like to meet?" He didn't say my name, and his voice was all business.

"Let's have dinner somewhere." He suggested a restaurant and we agreed to meet the next evening after work.

"Tomorrow then." I put a hint of warning in my voice.

"Yes. All right," he said and hung up. I wondered if my mother asked him who had called and, if she did, what he would have told her.

Next, I called up the man in whose living room I had stood naked. The phone rang many times. I was about to hang up, disappointed that there was not even a machine so I could hear his voice again, when a sleepy voice answered. I was caught by surprise and forgot my rehearsed line about meeting at a bakery I knew near his apartment for some sweetly indecent pastries. I hung up without saying anything.

THE WAITER takes our empty plates away. My father refills my glass. I have drunk two glasses of wine already and am starting to feel sleepy and complaisant. My father has already told me that he is not planning on seeing the woman again, and I am beginning to wonder what it is that I actually want my father to say.

He drums his fingers on the edge of the table. I can see that he is growing tired of being solicitous. He sought my opinion on the wine; he noticed that I had bangs cut; he remembered the name of my friend at work whom I was dating the last time we got together.

"I'm not with him anymore," I explain. "We thought it was a bad idea to date since we work together." I consider telling my father about the man, to let him know that I understand more about this world of affairs than he thinks. He would be shocked, outraged. Or would he? I'm not sure of anything anymore.

I let myself float outside the man's window again, move closer to peer inside. But this time I can't quite picture his face. What color are his eyes? They're green, I decide. But then I wonder if I am confusing them with my father's eyes.

"Someday, honey, you'll meet a guy who'll realize what a treasure you are." My father pats my knee.

"Just because he thinks I'm a treasure doesn't mean that he won't take me for granted." I take another sip of wine and watch over the rim of my glass for my father's response. I remember watching him at another table, our dining room table, where he sat across from my mother. She had just made some remark that I couldn't hear from where I perched on our front stairs, spying, as they had a romantic dinner alone with candles and wine. Earlier, my father had set up the television and VCR in my room and sent me upstairs to watch a movie. My father put down his glass and got up out of his chair. He knelt at my mother's feet and though I couldn't hear his words either I was sure that he was asking her to marry him again.

"Honey. Listen. It was nothing with that woman. It doesn't change the way I feel about your mother. I love your mother very much."

"But it makes everything such a lie," I say, my voice now catching with held-back tears. "What about our family, all the dinners, Sunday mornings around the breakfast table, the walks we love to take . . ." I falter and hold my hands out wide to him.

My father catches them and folds them closed in his own. "No. No. All of that is true. This doesn't change any of that." He is squeezing my hands hard. For the first time during this meal, I can see that I have upset him.

"But it didn't mean what I thought, did it?"

Right then the waiter appears with our check. My father lets go of my hands and reaches for his wallet. Neither of us says anything while we wait for the waiter to return with the credit-card slip. I don't repeat my question because I am afraid that my father will say I'm right.

THE NEXT DAY at work I ask my friend again about Mr. Sweetly Indecent.

"If you want to talk to him, call him up."

"Do you think I should?"

"It can't hurt."

"If we didn't work together, do you think things could have turned out differently with us?" We are in the photocopying room where in the midst of our affair my friend had once lifted my skirt and slid his fingers inside the elastic waist of my panty hose.

"Oh, hell. You'll meet someone who'll appreciate you. You deserve that. You really do."

I CALL the man up that night. He doesn't say anything for a moment when I tell him my name. I imagine him reviewing a long line of naked women standing in his living room. "That one," he finally picks me out of the crowd. Or maybe it's just that he's surprised to hear from me.

"I had a really nice time that night," I said. "I thought maybe we could get together again sometime."

"Well, I had a good time, too," he says, sounding sincere, "but I think that we should just leave it at that."

"I'm not saying that I want to start dating. I just thought that we could do something again."

"It was the kind of night that's better not repeated. I know. I've tried it before. The second time is always a disappointment."

"But I thought we got along so well." We had talked over dinner about our families; he told me how he was always trying to live up to the kind of man he thought his father wanted him to be. He had talked in faltering sentences, as though this were something that he was saying for the first time.

"We did get along," he says. "God! And you were so beautiful." He pauses and I know he's remembering that I really was beautiful. "I just want to preserve that memory of you standing in my living room, alone, without any other images cluttering it."

Yes, I want to tell him, I have preserved that image, too, but memories need refueling. I need to see you again to make sure that what I remembered is actually true. "Is this because I slept with you on the first night?"

"No. No. Nothing like that. Listen, it was a perfect night. Let's just both remember it that way."

As THE TRAIN pulls into the station, I spot my father waiting on the platform. I take my time gathering my things so I'm one of the last to exit. He hugs me without hesitation, as though our dinner had never happened. As we separate he tries to take my suitcase from me. It's just a small weekend bag and I resist, holding on to the shoulder strap. We have a tug-of-war.

"You're being ridiculous," my father says and yanks the strap from my grip. I trail behind him to the car and look out the window the whole way home.

That afternoon I sit at the kitchen table and watch my mother and father prune the rosebushes dotting the fence that separates our yard from the street. My mother selects a branch and shows my father where to cut. They work down the row quickly, efficient with their confidence in the new growth these efforts will bring. Behind them trails a wake of bald, stunted bushes and their snipped limbs lying crisscross on the ground beneath.

After they have finished cleaning up the debris, my father brings the lawn chairs out of the garage—he brings one for me, too, but I have retreated upstairs to my bedroom by this time and watch them from that window—and my mother appears with a pitcher of lemonade and glasses. My mother reclines in her chair, with my father at her side, and admires their handiwork. Her confidence that the world will obey her expectations makes her seem foolish to me. Or perhaps it is because every time I look at her I think of how she is being fooled.

On Sunday morning, my mother heads off to mass, and I am left alone in the house with my father. He sits with me at the kitchen table for a while, both of us flipping through the Sunday papers. I keep turning the pages, unable to find anything that can hold my attention. He's not really reading either. He is too busy waiting on me. He hands me the magazine and style sections without my even asking. He refills my coffee. When Georgie, our Labrador retriever, scratches at the door, he jumps up to let her out. When he sits back down, he gathers all the sections of the paper together, including the parts that I am looking at, and stacks them on one corner of the table. I look at him, breathe out a short note of exasperation.

"Are you ever going to forgive me?" he asks.

"Why aren't you going to see that woman again. Just because I caught you?"

He looks startled and answers slowly, as if he is just testing out this answer. "She didn't mean anything to me. It was like playing a game. It was fun but now it's over."

"Do you think that she expected to see you again?"

"No. She knew what kind of a thing it was. And I'm sure that she prefers it this way also. She has her own commitments to deal with."

"Maybe she does want to see you again. Maybe she felt like you had something really special together. Maybe she's hoping that you would leave Mom for her."

"Honey, when you get older you'll understand that there are a lot of different things that you can feel for another person and how it's important not to confuse them. I love your mother and I'm very devoted to her. Nothing is going to change that."

My father sits with me a few minutes more, and when

there doesn't seem to be anything else to say, he stands up and wanders off. I realize that if I had told my father about the man during our dinner, he would have understood what kind of a thing that was before I did.

When my mother gets back, she joins me at the kitchen table.

"Do you want to talk about something, honey? You seem so sad." I look at my mother and the tears that have been welling in my eyes all weekend threaten to spill over.

"Daddy says you're having boy trouble."

I shake my head no, unable to speak.

My mother suggests that we take the dog out for a walk, just the two of us, so we can catch up. She gathers our coats, calls Georgie, and we head out the door. "I don't even know what's going on in your life since you've moved out. It's strange," she says, "I used to know what you did every evening, who you were going out with, what clothes you chose to wear each day. Now I have no idea how you spend your time. It was different when you were at college. I could imagine you in class, or at the library, or sitting around your dorm room with your roommate. Sometimes I used to stop whatever I was doing and think about you. She's probably just heading off to the cafeteria for breakfast right now, I would tell myself."

We are walking down our street toward the harbor.

"But you know that I go to work every day. You know what my apartment looks like. It's the same now."

"No, it's not," she says. "It's really all your own life. You support yourself, buy all your own clothes, decide if and when to have breakfast. And somehow, I don't feel right imagining what your day is like. It's not really my business anymore."

"I don't mind, Mom, if you want to know what I'm doing." We have reached the harbor and my mother is bending over the dog to let her off the lead, so I'm not sure if she hears me. She pulls a tennis ball out of her pocket and Georgie begins to dance backward. My mother starts walking to the water. I stay where I am and look off across the harbor. On the opposite shore, some boats have been pulled up onto the beach for the winter just above the high-tide mark. They rest on the side of their hulls and look as if they've been forgotten, as if they will never be put back in the water again.

My mother turns toward me, holding the tennis ball up high over her head. Georgie is prancing and barking in front of her. "You know what I love about dogs? It's so easy to make them happy. You just pet them or give them a biscuit or show them a ball and they always wag their tails." She throws the ball into the water and Georgie goes racing after it.

My mother's eagerness to oblige surprises me. I think of her dancing with men in that club in West Berlin. I had always imagined her as acting very primly, holding the men away from her with stiff, straight arms. Perhaps she wasn't that way at all. Maybe she leaned into these men, only drawing back to toss her head in laughter at the jokes they whispered in her ear.

"Mom, what made you go out with Dad when you worked in that club? You didn't go out with many of the men that you met there, did you?"

"Your father was the only one I accepted, though I certainly had many offers."

"Did he seem more respectable?"

"Oh, he came on like a playboy as much as the next one."

"Then why did you say yes?"

"Well, somehow he seemed like he didn't quite believe his whole act. Though he wouldn't say that if you asked him. I guess I felt I understood something about him that he didn't even know about himself. So he went about seducing me, all the while feeling like he had the upper hand, and I would go along, knowing that I had a trick up my sleeve, too."

She isn't looking at me as she says this. She is turned toward the water, though I know that she is not looking at that either. She is watching herself as a young woman twirling around a room with my young father. They dance together well; I have seen them dance before, and this memory brings such a pleased private smile to her lips that I don't say anything that would contradict her.

I AM QUIET during dinner. My parents treat me like I am sick or have just suffered some great loss. My mother won't let me help her serve the food. My father pushes seconds on me, saying that I look too skinny. "Maybe I should take you out to dinner more often," he says.

I look up from my heaping plate of food, half expecting him to wink at me.

"That's right. You two met for dinner this week. See, honey, that's just the kind of thing I was talking about. It's nice that you and your father can meet and have dinner together. Like two friends."

My parents tell stories back and forth about me when I was young; many stories I have heard before. Usually I enjoy these conversations. I listen to them describe this precocious girl and the things she has done that I can't even remember, only interrupting to ask in an incredulous and proud tone, "I really did that?" I am always willing to believe anything my parents tell me, so curious am I to understand the continuum of how I came to be the woman I am. Tonight, while these memories seem to console my parents, I can only hear them as nostalgic, and they remind me of everything that has been recently forsaken.

After dinner I insist on doing the dishes. I splash around

in the kitchen sink, clattering the plates dangerously in their porcelain bed. I pick up a serving platter, one from my mother's set of good china inherited from my grandmother, and consider dropping it to the floor. I have trouble picturing myself actually doing this. I can only imagine it as far as my fingers loosening from the edges of the platter and it sliding down their length, but then in my mind's eye instead of the platter falling swiftly, it floats and hovers the way a feather would from one of the peacocks pictured on the china's face. I have no trouble picturing the aftermath once it lands: my mother rushing in at the noise with my father a few steps behind, not sure if he must concern himself, and she angry at my carelessness. I imagine yelling back at her. I would tell her that it's no use. Old china, manicured lawns, a happy dog: these things don't offer any guarantee.

I stand there holding the platter high above the kitchen floor, imagining the consequences with trepidation and relief, as if this is what the weekend has been leading up to, and with one brief burst of courage I can put it behind me. I stand considering and strain to hear my parents' voices in the dining room, thinking their conversation might offer me some direction. I put the platter down and peek around the open kitchen door. A pantry separates me from the dining room. I can see them: they are talking, but I can't make out their words.

They are both leaning forward. My mother cradles her chin in the palm of her hand. Abruptly, she lifts her head, sits up tall, and points at my father. His arms are folded in front of him, and he looks down and shakes his head. I am reminded again of that dinner of theirs that I spied on years ago, but this time what I remember is the righteousness of my mother's posture as she sat across from my father and tossed off remarks and the guilty urgency of my father's movements as he sank to his knees at her feet, and how there was something slightly orchestrated about their behavior, as though their exchange had a long history to it. And the next thing I remember makes me tiptoe away, as I did when I was a child, aware that I had witnessed a private moment between my parents not meant for my eyes. What I remember now is how many years ago my mother had reached down her hand and pulled my father up and kept pulling him in toward herself so that she could hold him close.

At the Bottom
of the Lake

ᘒ

LUCY WAS in the kitchen making cheese puffs for the cocktail party. She'd left them for last. Baking with the cabin's wood-burning stove required precisely timed shiftings of the pan in the oven. After three minutes, she moved the puffs from left to right. When the kitchen timer rang again, she flipped them around and pulled them to the oven's front.

From outside, she heard a loud splash, and then Sam, her fiancé, called her to the window. His naked figure was climbing up the ladder to the dock. "I think the one that got away just bumped against my leg," he said. One of the stories she'd told him from her summers here with her father was about an immense bass that had pulled her fishing rod from her hands.

Lucy said, "Sure it did, Sam."

"That bastard scared the shit out of me," he said, slicing right past her sarcasm. He shimmied a towel down his back. "I should get my pole. Wouldn't your dad be surprised if young blood here landed the big one?" Sam smiled as if imagining the reluctant admiration on Lucy's father's face.

He draped the towel over his neck and headed up the path toward the cabin.

"You better put some clothes on," Lucy called, "or else he and Victoria are going to be in for an even bigger surprise."

"You got that right," Sam said and began strutting up the walk. When he reached the window where Lucy stood, he puckered his lips and pressed them to the screen. "Do you promise to love me and cherish me and say flattering things about my dick until death does its part?"

She rolled her eyes. "It's 'death do *us* part,' not 'does its part.'"

Now he mashed his face against the screen. "Do you promise or not?"

"Would you get dressed, please," she said, turning away. "I could use some help, you know."

"What time are people coming?" Sam called as he walked through the living room to the bedroom.

"For the party?"

"Is there any other reason people are coming?"

"Jesus Christ," Lucy muttered under her breath. "I already told you," she yelled. "Six-thirty." Checking her watch, she added, "Which is in about an hour and a half."

THIS COCKTAIL PARTY was in honor of her father's return to the family cabin on the lake. It had been eight years since his last visit, and Lucy was determined that everything this weekend would go smoothly. Which was not going to be easy, considering that her stepmother was coming, too. Lucy suspected that Victoria's only purpose in joining her husband was to thwart any campaigns for future trips. For no other reason could Lucy imagine her venturing away from the deep-pile carpeting and muted whites with which she surrounded herself in their Park Avenue apartment.

Lucy had been nine when her father married Victoria. Victoria pouted through a few summers on the lake before finally announcing that she hated the cabin; she hated that there was no telephone or running water or electricity; she hated that the only way to reach the place was by a launch which fetched you at a distant parking lot, and that Walt, the caretaker, was frequently out fishing so you had to call again and again before reaching him to make the arrangement; she hated the oppressive quiet, and when the loons began their mournful calling, she hated that, too. Lucy and her younger sister, Sarah, had expected Victoria to add that she especially hated them, but that went without saying.

All the things her stepmother hated, Lucy loved. As a child, she would convince herself that this life was the only one that existed. The happiness she felt at this far-off place stood alone, distinct and irrefutable.

Lucy's father continued bringing Lucy and Sarah up to the lake without Victoria, but the trips got shorter and less frequent, and when Sarah finally entered college and the mandatory two weeks in the summer stipulated by the visitation agreement ended, her father stopped coming altogether. And for a while the cabin stood empty.

Five years ago, Lucy had returned on her own. For the first few summers she brought friends along, and then Sam began coming with her. Now it was up to her to perform all the chores that the primitive life at the cabin required. As she chopped wood for the stove or scrubbed the smoky film from the glass casings of the lanterns or washed the laundry in the tub off the dock, she would think of her father and the methodical ways he'd moved through these tasks, and she would feel like him. In the mornings, she would get up early to start the stove for breakfast, working quietly so as not to wake anyone, and then take a cup of coffee outside to watch the shadows draw back across the water and the dew steam upward in spirals between the trees, and she would know that same peacefulness that she'd seen on her father's face when, as a child, finally waking, she would join him on the porch.

For so many years, Lucy had claimed that she didn't understand her father, how he could prefer spoiled, petulant Victoria over Lucy's gracious and capable mother, how he could then choose his new wife over his own two kids, how he could turn his back on this place he'd visited as a boy with his own father—she was astonished to suddenly discover this kinship of feeling. And she began to imagine ways to get him back here.

So when Lucy called her father to say that she and Sam had gotten engaged and he asked her what she wanted for a present, she told him simply: *For you to spend a weekend with us on the lake.* To her surprise, he'd said yes. She'd held her breath for a moment, waiting for him to add, "So long as it's OK with Vicky." But he hadn't. They'd discussed some possible dates, and he'd said that he would call her back once he firmed up the details. After the phone call ended, Lucy had remained sitting, dizzy with hope, her hand still resting on the receiver.

SHE HAD BEGUN preparing another tray of cheese puffs when she heard Sam walk into the kitchen and stop. Before he could speak, she pointed out that the sink was full of dishes, and that the mixers still needed to be put out.

"You always complain about how much water I use when I do the dishes."

She measured out another dollop of dough. "Then don't use so much," she said.

A holding tank supplied water for the bathroom and the kitchen sink, but filling this tank was a long, complicated process involving starting the balky generator, opening a

series of taps, and working the pump. "That's why it's important to conserve water," she'd explained more than once. Sam
hadn't yet come to see the inconveniences of life at the cabin
as part of its charm.

After loading up the oven once more, Lucy sank down
into a chair and said: "I wish *I* had time to go swimming."

"Oh, why don't you go jump in a lake," Sam said.

She smiled faintly.

"So, how're you doing?" he asked.

She looked blankly around the kitchen. Most of the food
for the party was laid out on the table. Moistened dish towels
covered the vegetables for the crudités to prevent their drying out. The cream cheese–artichoke dip was waiting in the
fridge, and the crackers were already in the living room.

Lucy trapped her lip between her teeth. "You think my
father will remember that Mom always made that artichoke
dip?"

"Does it matter if he does?"

"Sam." Lucy's tone made it clear that it did matter, and
that he damn well knew it.

He leaned against the counter. "All right. From the one
time I met him, I would say that he is not the type of man
who pays attention to things like dip. And from everything
you've told me about him, it doesn't sound like he remem-
bers much of anything from life with Mom."

Lucy realized that he was right, and that this was not the
answer she wanted. She shook her head and covered her face
with her hands. Her voice, when she spoke, came out muffled. "I know I'm being a little crazy."

Sam crouched in front of her so he could look up at her
face. He wiggled a fingertip between the wedge of her fingers. "Are you going to be OK?" he asked softly.

Her hands parted; she raised her arms and then let them
drop to her sides. "And what if I'm not?" she asked.

"Then I'll hug you and make you better," he said, his voice rising in a question.

Looking down at him, Lucy saw the reassurance in his wide smile, in his warm eyes. So far, Sam had remained magnanimous amid Lucy's frenzied preparations for this visit. He'd helped her clean out the cabin and burn all the rubbish; he'd amused himself during the hours she spent sorting through closets and darning the ancient bedspreads. Last night she couldn't sleep, and he'd held her and whispered in her ear that he loved her, that he would love her forever, and Lucy, rigid in his arms, had reflected unhappily what a reckless promise that was.

She wished she could believe him now—his certainty that he could provide a sufficient substitute for whatever else she sought. She grabbed a handful of his blond curls and shook his head gently. He leaned forward for her to scratch his neck, but she put her hands on his shoulders and pushed him away.

"Let me up," she said. "I have to turn my puffs."

THE WARNING TOOT of the launch's horn announced the arrival of Lucy's father and Victoria. Lucy was on her last tray, so Sam walked down to the dock to greet them. She heard him call out a welcome, and she went to the window and looked out. She'd rebuilt the dock since her father's last visit, and she was anxious to see his reaction to it. But he was leaning down over Victoria and gave no sign of noticing.

Lucy watched her father assist his wife out of the launch, handing her over to Sam as gently as if the two men were moving a delicate and valuable piece of furniture. She could hear her father saying something, and Victoria turned to shake Sam's hand. Lucy couldn't make out her stepmother's words either, but she guessed from the stagy lilt of her aristocratic voice, the dramatic stops and starts, that she was describing affronts and upheavals.

In the stern of the boat, Lucy's dad was busy gathering together the luggage. Sam turned to him and extended his hand in greeting. A canvas bag was pressed into it. The timer rang, as if giving voice to Lucy's dismay.

When they all burst into the kitchen, she was in the midst of rotating the last tray. She clumsily jerked her hands out of the oven, knocking one forearm against the edge of the cast-iron door.

"You should be more careful," her father admonished.

With her uninjured arm, she clutched him in a hasty hug, and then they hustled around trying to wrestle some ice from the ancient trays. Sam went to the bathroom to look for first-aid cream. Victoria chimed in: "I once remember hearing at a party that one can prevent the skin from blistering by rubbing the burnt area roughly against one's hair."

Lucy raised her arm and gave a few skeptical rubs. It hurt like hell. She wondered if her stepmother had just made this up.

"What's all this?" Lucy's father asked, pointing to the table of food.

"I thought we should celebrate," she said brightly. "I invited everyone who's around to come over for drinks."

"Oh, good," Victoria chirped. "You can use my tray." As an engagement present, Victoria had sent Lucy a large silver tray with an appeal for eternal happiness engraved on the back.

"Actually, I didn't bring it." Lucy waved a hand around the rustic kitchen, indicating the mismatched crockery lining the open shelves and the collection of blue-enamel pots hanging over the stove. "It doesn't exactly go with what's here." Her stepmother stared at her. "I really like it, though," she said, trying to pump her voice full of enthusiasm.

"Well, you should. It's from Tiffany's."

"Right. I recognized the box. You got my note, didn't you?"

Thank God, thought Lucy, that I got that note in the mail. She and her stepmother didn't fight about the big issues anymore—perhaps because they realized that many of the things they would have said to each other could cause irreparable damage. But now forgetting to send a thank-you note or overlooking a birthday could lead to months of silence and coldness.

"Well." Victoria humphed and sat down.

Lucy kept glancing over to her father. The only times she had seen him in almost a year were on television news programs—as a senior partner in a large New York law firm, he was occasionally enlisted to offer legal opinions on high-publicity cases—and she was having difficulty reconciling his appearances there with this ruddy-faced figure standing in the kitchen. On TV, with his hair tamed and the redness of his skin toned down with makeup, he'd looked judicious and composed, like the sort of man you could reason with.

He crouched down to peer at the underbelly of the water-holding tank. "Hardly any rust." He rapped it with his knuckles. "This tank is almost thirty years old."

"That's absolutely fascinating, Frank," said Victoria. "God, I'd forgotten how miserable that drive is. I feel like I've been up for days." She turned to her stepdaughter and looked her over. "You've lost weight."

Lucy glanced down at herself and shrugged.

Sam, having reappeared with some hydrogen peroxide, seconded Victoria's opinion. "That's what I keep telling her. She runs around too much. Can't get her to sit down."

Lucy's father gestured to the bottle Sam held. "What's that going to do? She didn't cut herself."

Sam met Frank Baldwin's gaze. He hesitated for a moment, and his eyes narrowed. Only when Lucy touched his arm did he look down, smiling resolutely. "It was the only thing I could find," he explained in a quiet voice.

"Yes, you're looking very well," Victoria said as she turned away.

Victoria announced that if she was going to be in any kind of humor to socialize, she needed to lie down for a bit. "Any chance you've replaced those horrible camp beds?"

Lucy shook her head.

Victoria sighed. "I suppose I could sleep on a bed of nails right now." She stood up and walked off, calling back over her shoulder, "Bring me a drink, would you, Frank dear?"

Seeing her chance to have her father alone, Lucy spoke up. "I thought maybe we could walk around a bit before the party. We have an hour or so. I want to show you some things."

"Yes, I'd like to know why you moved the dock."

"You noticed."

"Of course I noticed." He picked up the suitcases. "Just give me a minute. You did remember to get some gin, I hope?"

"You think I'm crazy? It's in the living room," Lucy said. "You'll have to use this ice." She dislodged a few more pieces from the metal tray and placed them in a glass. "The Sweeneys are bringing more for the party."

Once she and Sam were alone, Lucy shook her head and gave a disbelieving laugh. "See what I mean about her?"

"Don't you two even kiss hello?" Sam asked.

"Please," she said in a sarcastic voice, as though this fact were nothing compared to other transgressions. "We used to. I can't remember who stopped first."

He crossed his arms and smiled. "She's sort of charming in an odd way. That voice. She's like some old society maven in a novel." He looked at Lucy and cocked his head. "You know, you two kind of look alike."

She made a face. "No, we don't."

Victoria's upswept coif was blond, at least it had been for years, and her eyes were a milky blue. Lucy's hair was dark and unruly, and the blue of her eyes was many shades deeper.

Sam persisted. "Something about the shape of your faces or your expressions. I don't know. You both have these large eyes like children do," he said, widening his own eyes.

Lucy dismissed this observation with a shake of her head.

She began wiping off the counter. For a moment there during the hectic greeting, the weekend seemed to be heading off on a miserable trajectory, and the words *It's no use; it's too late* were spinning wildly through Lucy's head. But now everything seemed all right again. She would get her chance to show her father what good care she'd taken of the place in his absence. Victoria was settled with her drink. And Sam had come up behind her and was wrapping his arms around her waist. "Of course, you're much prettier," he whispered into her ear. Lucy leaned into him. "I can't believe he's really here," she said. "Mom and Sarah were betting that Victoria would make a scene at the last minute and they wouldn't come. But I knew he would make it. He loves this place. I *know* he does." Her voice became dreamy. "Wait till you hear him talk about it. He knows all the history." She turned her head toward Sam. "How each family ended up here. The year each cabin was built. Christ, he's had a hand in blazing most of the trails. He knows all the names of the birds." She trailed off.

Sam nestled his face into her neck. "You know that stuff, too, Luce. He handed all that stuff down to you." He paused and then said quietly, "And you know, honey, that may have to be good enough."

Lucy could have explained that having her father here was the closest she could feel to having her father back, but she didn't. She closed her eyes and breathed in the peppermint scent of Sam's hair. He smelled of the Dr. Castille's soap her family had been using to bathe in the lake for years. Pressing her nose to his hair, she thought how nice it was to discover this familiar scent on Sam, to feel her past and present mingling together.

LUCY AND her father walked down to the dock. From its edge, the entire length of the lake was visible. At one end was the narrow sand beach where Lucy had learned to swim. On the other end, a bald cliff face jutted above a slope of woods that reached far out toward the lake's center. The hike up to that cliff took half a day. When Lucy was a child, her father would have to carry her on his back for the last steep leg. Between the beach and cliff, pine and maple and birch trees formed a rippling blanket of green, rising and falling, a silhouette of the irregular shoreline. Pale clouds of mist hung in the valleys between the hills, and the late afternoon sun reflected off the water, catching the underside of the leaves to fill the woods with an invisible shimmering light.

The beauty of this place still surprised Lucy. She wouldn't have thought that something so familiar could seem so beautiful.

Her father jumped up and down on the dock a few times and frowned at the bounce of the platform.

"It's supposed to do that," she told him.

When Lucy had first come back to the lake, the wooden platform of their old dock was gone. She wondered if someone had stolen the lumber for firewood, but Walt explained that after many winters of the water's freezing, the ice had finally wrenched the platform from its stone crib, and then when the lake melted, the wood had floated away. Before rebuilding the dock, Lucy had Walt take her around in the launch to look at all the other docks, and she was eager to demonstrate to her father the superiority of this new design. She remembered that, in her childhood, one of his greatest pleasures was the discovery of faults in other people's sewer systems, or kitchen stoves, or the way they stacked their firewood.

"You've got to have a look at this," she said.

They both lay down and peered over the dock's edge. The new platform rested on a hemlock log which hung from cables off two large boulders. She explained how this design allowed the platform to rise and fall with the freezing of the lake to protect it from the twisting of the ice. Floating her hand in the water, she imitated the movement of the log. She turned to her father and smiled.

"You built this?"

"Me, Sam, Walt, and the kid he had working for him last summer."

Lucy's father patted the log a few times and then hopped to his feet. "You'll be lucky if it lasts three years. You can't hang all this weight on one log and expect it to last very long. Especially when you've got the log sitting in the water half the time." He wiped his hands on his pant leg.

"But that's just it." Lucy stood up also. "This way the log rises with the water." She touched her damp fingers to her face, her warm cheeks.

"Well, I guess you're in charge now," her father said, sounding a little regretful. "You'll want to do things your own way." He walked down the bank to where the old dock had been. Under the water sat the empty crib of piled stones.

"Do you know how long it took for your grandfather to collect all those rocks? You can't find rocks that size around here. He brought those stones in from the old quarry in a wheelbarrow." Lucy's father pointed in the direction of the quarry, which lay a half mile from there. "Do you know how many trips it took him?"

He was quiet for a moment, and then he posed his question again, making Lucy realize that he expected an answer.

"Ten?" she said in a small voice.

"Seventeen," he said, and then he turned and started up the path.

The rest of the walk felt like a hurried job interview, with Lucy listing off the repairs she had done, and her father posing an occasional question. She showed him the new shelter she and Sam had built for the woodpile, and the siding they'd replaced on the outside of a back bedroom.

"Where'd you find this siding?" he asked, running his hand across the rough-cut pine.

Lucy hesitated, unsure if she had made another blunder. "It's from a lumberyard near Conway," she said.

He leaned forward and, closing his eyes, smelled the wood. "It's hard to find," he said.

Lucy's father paused on the porch for a moment before going inside. He took a breath as though he were about to say something and then sighed and walked over to the rail. He looked through the trees toward the water. The Sweeneys were just setting off from their dock across the lake.

"God, I haven't rowed in . . ." He paused, trying to recall how long.

"Eight years," Lucy supplied. "You'll remember how."

"Oh, I know I'll remember. I just don't have those muscles anymore." He smiled at something and shook his head. "A few years ago, Vicky gave me a rowing machine for Christmas. I think I've used it twice."

"It's hardly the same thing," Lucy said.

"That's what I told her." He rested his elbows on the railing. In the falling dusk, the loons had begun calling to each other across the water, one echoing the other, as if to say *Are you there? Still there?* The only other sound was the quiet splash of the Sweeneys' oars. The evening was darkening quickly now as the sun fell behind the hill.

"I'm glad you've taken an interest in this place," he said, still looking out. "You're doing a good job with it."

Taken an interest, Lucy repeated these words in her head. People take an interest in stamps or the stock market. This cabin was the only place that had ever felt to her like home. "Well, I couldn't let it just go to ruin," she said. "I've got too many memories here."

"So do I," her father answered, and she could see, even in the long shadow of evening, how his face looked pained as he said this.

When they went back inside, Sam and Victoria were sitting in the living room. Lucy's stepmother had changed into beige silk slacks and a black tunic. A beige sweater draped her shoulders, and a black lizard mule swung from her foot. Victoria had always been a stunning dresser, the kind of woman who thought of dressing well as part of the social obligation of her background. When Lucy was growing up, the other women had worn their old blue jeans or practical shapeless cotton skirts while at the lake, but Victoria had loafed around in linen trousers and skinny sleeveless turtlenecks that showed off her slender arms.

As a child, Lucy would accompany her stepmother on shopping trips to Madison Avenue. Victoria would pick out piles of lavish dresses for Lucy to try on. After narrowing the selection down to three or four, she would offer to buy her one. Lucy remembered being embarrassed by how much she wanted these dresses. Finally, after long deliberation she would make her choice. While the saleslady rang the dress up and packed it away in tissue paper, she might beam at Lucy and tell her what a lucky girl she was to have such a lovely dress, and Lucy, shyly, would put her hand in her stepmother's, feeling for a moment that indeed she was very lucky. When she got home, her mother would take the dress out of her suitcase, unwrapping it from its layers of tissue paper. She would finger the fabric and examine the label, muttering, "Ridiculous."

For a while, Lucy had defended Victoria to her mother. Her stepmother's clothes, her pale taste in furnishings, the way she would swirl the ice cubes in her cocktail while she asked Lucy questions about her classmates, had all seemed very glamorous to her. What Lucy hadn't expected was that Victoria would grow tired of her stepdaughters, that she would with increasing frequency arrange to have the girl from a neighboring apartment baby-sit during the weekend visits so that she and Lucy's father could still go out to dinner, that she wouldn't have as much fun shopping for a teenager who had tastes of her own.

Victoria asked Sam to mix her another drink. "Not too much tonic, please," she requested, and then, as though someone had asked her to explain herself, she added, "You've only got one bottle. I don't want to use it all up."

"There's more in the kitchen," Lucy said flatly.

"Well, we've got to make it through the weekend."

"Yup," Lucy whispered into Sam's ear. He stood at the sideboard, pouring Victoria's drink. He pointed to the glass and shrugged. "It's fine," she said quietly. Over her shoulder, she asked her father what he would like.

Victoria broke in. "She's so organized, Sam. It's really quite incredible. She's prepared for anything."

"Scotch or whiskey," Lucy's father said. "Whatever you've got. Straight up is fine if you're low on ice."

"Your mother was very organized, wasn't she?"

Lucy handed her father his drink. "She still is," she said, turning to her stepmother.

"Yes. Of course." Victoria nodded. When Sam handed over her drink, she touched his arm and called him a lamb.

Lucy lit some more lanterns and poured herself a glass of wine. She looked around for a place to sit. Sam had positioned himself in a chair in the corner, as though he didn't want his presence to interfere with this reunion. She chose a seat on the sofa next to the fireplace and kept glancing over at him, trying to catch his eye so that she could signal for him to join her. Didn't he know that she wanted him, that she needed him at her side? She would never have had the courage to go through with this weekend if Sam weren't with her. Until she met him, she hadn't understood that another person could share the burden of your life. Lucy and Sarah, during their childhood visits to their father, hadn't even been able to meet each other's eye. There, they would have seen their own sadness mirrored, a recognition that would only confirm this grief as being as real and lonely as they feared.

Victoria tapped her fingernail against her glass. "Sam was telling me about his job designing products," she said. "I didn't realize that someone actually designs products. I know, of course, that *someone* has to come up with the idea, but I never thought that there was an actual person whose job it was to do it. It's really very impressive. Your boss comes to you and says"—she put on a deep, commanding voice—" 'Sam, we need a can opener.' And, presto, he designs a can opener." Her hand flicked upward. "And perhaps it's a very beautiful can opener, the very essence of can openers."

Sam looked baffled, as though he were unsure whether he was being mocked or flattered. If he had been sitting next to Lucy, she could have told him that this commentary meant nothing; it was just her stepmother's way of filling up the time. Victoria could talk to a wall, her husband had bragged.

Lucy's father shifted in his seat to look out the window. "The Sweeneys should be here soon," he commented.

"Pat and Henry Sweeney," Victoria said. "I remember them. He was caught with his hand up the baby-sitter's shirt one summer."

Lucy glanced at Sam and rolled her eyes. "That was just gossip," she said.

"Absolutely," agreed Victoria.

IN THE MIDST of greeting people and fetching their drinks, Lucy noticed that her stepmother had commandeered Sam to sit by her side. He'd pulled up a bench next to the large overstuffed chair where Victoria sat and was positioned by her knees like a disciple. Lucy didn't want to think about what her stepmother could be telling him. She was on her third drink now, having sent Sam back to the bar another time.

Sometimes Victoria's chatter slid onto a less inconsequential plane: the story of her first husband's death, perhaps, or her suicide attempt; the way Lucy's father had glued her life back together again. And Victoria would be sure to tell Sam about all her attempts at befriending Lucy and her sister, the shopping trips, the matinees. She'd tell him how her first husband couldn't have children, and all she ever wanted was for Frank's girls to like her. If she'd had enough to drink, this revelation could make her weep.

Lucy fetched the tray of cheese puffs and began to pass them around the party. Her father was chatting with some of his old friends. A number of people had seen his television appearances, and he was entertaining them with stories about various infamous defendants.

She made her way over to Victoria and Sam.

"I'm sure they're delicious, Lucy, dear, but I couldn't eat a thing." Victoria had her hand on the tray and was pulling it down toward her lap. "Sam. You must have one. I insist. Lucy's a gourmet cook. Another talent she inherited from her mother. Me?" She released the tray to touch her chest. "The only thing I know how to make is reservations." She laughed heartily and Sam laughed, too. He selected a cheese puff. "They're delicious," he said, his mouth full of food.

"Could you help me for a minute, please?" Lucy said, widening her eyes.

In the kitchen, she put the tray down and turned to face Sam. "You're supposed to be on my side," she said, crossing her arms.

"What are you talking about?"

"Why have you been sitting with her all night? You should be getting to know my father, not Victoria."

"Lucy." His head deflated to his chest. "What was I going to do? She asked me to sit next to her. And your father's catching up with all his old cronies. I thought that was the point? Have him reconnect with his pals. Entice him to start coming here again. Besides, I have years of getting to know your father to look forward to." His tone, when he said this, did not suggest that he *did* actually look forward to this prospect.

"What do you mean by that?" Lucy asked.

"He's been pretty cold to me, don't you think?" Sam nonchalantly popped a carrot stick into his mouth as though they were discussing a work acquaintance of Lucy's or a college friend.

"He hardly knows you," Lucy said. And then seeing the affront in Sam's face at this explanation, she added, "It takes him a while to warm up to people."

"I don't know why you always make out Victoria as the villain," Sam said between bites. "She's been asking all about you, and she can't stop complimenting you." He smiled wanly. "Though I guess the business about bringing up your mother all the time isn't great."

"No. It isn't." She looked down, shaking her head.

He laid his hand across her hip. "I'm sorry. I know Victoria's been really awful to you. But your father." He breathed a weary, astonished sigh. "He's to blame, too. He let Victoria get in the way of your relationship. He could have stood up to her more."

"You know, this is my fucking life you're dissecting so casually!" Lucy found that she was holding back tears. Sam looked as surprised as if she had struck him. "Why can't you just be on my side?" she pleaded.

"Lucy. Lucy." He took her in his arms. "Of course, I'm on your side." He smoothed her hair, pulling it away from her face. "But aren't I entitled to my own view?"

She didn't say anything, but in her head she was telling him that no, he wasn't.

When they went back into the living room, Victoria looked up briefly and smiled as though she had some idea of the distress she'd caused in the kitchen. Lucy steered Sam over to her father and introduced him to the men standing there. The conversation had moved on to an old argument about running in telephone lines to the cabins.

"Not for business calls or the gals telephoning each other up, but what if there's an emergency?" Mr. Langley was saying. "Thank God, we've never had to put the flare system to a test, but I wouldn't want to be the guy who finds out that it doesn't work."

"Why shouldn't the flares work?" Mr. Baldwin queried. "Walt sees the signal, one for ambulance, two for fire, he makes the call."

"Walt!" Mr. Sweeney exclaimed, waving his hand in dismissal. "Who knows what he's up to all day long."

"I'm with Frank," said Mr. Hamlin. "If it isn't broken, then why fix it. That's my motto."

"Why wouldn't you just use a cell phone in an emergency," Sam said. His comment was met with blank faces. "A cellular phone. I think you can even rent them pretty reasonably." Mr. Langley raised his eyebrows. "If you're worried about the flares not working, that is, then just get a cell phone," Sam said, sucking the final bit of wind from the argument.

There was a long, still pause.

"But how are you going to charge it?" Mr. Baldwin touched a finger to Sam's chest. "You need electricity to charge those phones." And the sails were filled once more.

"That's right," chimed in Mr. Hamlin. "And they're very unreliable."

"Cell phones!" With another wave of his hand, Mr. Sweeney dismissed them, too. "That's why I'm in favor of running in the damn telephone lines. It's not progress, it's safety I'm talking about."

"It's on the agenda for a vote at the meeting," Hamlin said.

"Yeah, Frank, you're going to come back for the meeting in August, aren't you?" Langley said. "The only lawyer on the lake these days is Baker's son-in-law, and he's hopeless."

"Hopeless," Sweeney echoed.

"I'll see." Frank Baldwin glanced at his daughter, who stood a step outside this conversation. "We'll see."

LUCY WAS WATCHING Victoria. By her count, her stepmother was on her fourth drink, and she looked to be caught between trying to maintain her dignity and the loosening effects of the alcohol. Throughout the party, Lucy had noticed the gradual slackening in the lordly cock of her stepmother's chin.

Perched on the edge of the bench, Mrs. Hamlin was quietly talking with her. She was leaning forward, her expression compassionate, as though it were condolences she whispered in her companion's ear. Victoria's hands wrapped more firmly around her glass.

She closed her eyes for a long moment and waved her hand in front of her, shooing Mrs. Hamlin away. The woman sat up and looked around the party for another witness to this peculiar behavior. And it was Lucy's gaze she caught just as Lucy was looking away.

She took a step closer to her father. Sam was on her other side, and she clasped his hand in hers. If Mrs. Hamlin wanted to suggest to someone that Victoria seemed tired, or some other euphemism for being drunk, she would have to take it up with somebody other than Lucy. She was busy with her fiancé. She had her own commitments now.

She glanced up to see Mrs. Hamlin heading toward her.

Victoria solved the problem by calling loudly across the room. "Frank. Frank," she beckoned.

"Excuse me," said Mr. Baldwin, and he went to his wife.

The men's gaze followed him. Sam's hand shifted nervously in Lucy's grip. He cleared his throat and said, "Um . . . Lucy and I have been training for the rowing race."

Mr. Sweeney glanced back. "Oh?" he said, raising his eyebrows.

"I still can't quite get the hang of hand rotation," Sam continued. He released Lucy's fingers and began circling his arms in a pantomime of rowing. Soon he had the men's attention. They took turns demonstrating their techniques.

Lucy felt strangely calm as she watched her father bend over Victoria.

Her stepmother's voice rose. Lucy understood the word "glasses." Her father said something and put his hand to Victoria's elbow. She shook him off.

"Yes, that's what I said. I want my reading glasses." She was pointing to the shelf of books above the old pine table. "There's a poem I've been trying to remember. I want to show it to Lucy."

Lucy glanced at Sam at the mention of her name, but he didn't seem to have heard, so intently was he listening to Mr. Langley as he stressed the importance of building up calluses. She inclined her head as though she, too, were concerned with this subject.

But then Victoria was calling her name, and Mrs. Hamlin had appeared at her shoulder and was whispering in her ear, "Just go along with her, dear. See if you can get her to bed."

Lucy took a step backward and now Sam turned to her. She shook her head at him as though he were the one who was creating the fuss.

"What is it, Victoria?" Exasperation sharpened her words.

"Yeats. I'm sure it's Yeats." Victoria closed one eye and pointed to a book on the shelf. "The blue one, I think." She turned to Lucy's father. "Will you please fetch me my glasses? They're on the bureau. You know I can't make out a word without them."

"Victoria," her husband said in a hushed tone. "I don't think you should read right now."

"Frank, why can't you just do what I ask? It's a simple thing." She lowered her brow to her hand and wagged her head back and forth. "You're always telling me what I can't do. I'm not a child, for heaven's sake."

Victoria pointed again. "The blue one." Lucy sighed and walked over to the shelf. "No, not that one. Right. That's it. Bring it here."

Sam, having detached himself finally from the rowing conversation, hovered next to Victoria's chair. His body looked tensed, ready for action, as though he might be called upon to perform some athletic feat. Everyone had quieted slightly in deference to the drama that was developing before them. Lucy's stepmother reached out a hand to pull Sam closer. "You should hear this, too. It's a lesson about marriage."

"This is ridiculous," muttered Lucy.

Once Victoria's glasses were in place, she thumbed through the pages, holding the book closer and then farther away. She found the page she was seeking and lowered her face to the small print. She moved her glasses a little farther down her nose, and then looked up, smiling sheepishly. "Here, Sam. You read it. Read it to Lucy. This one. 'When You Are Old.'"

Sam looked at Lucy, who shook her head and shrugged. He cleared his throat and glanced quickly around the room. Everyone had given up feigning conversation at this point. Sam raised his eyebrows and scowled and then smiled dimly, as though trying to locate some appropriate expression in which to settle his face. Clearing his throat once more, he began to read:

When You Are Old

When you are old and gray and full of sleep,
And nodding by the fire, take down this book,
  (Here, Victoria nodded.)
And slowly read, and dream of the soft look
Your eyes had once, and of their shadows deep;

How many loved your moments of glad grace,
  (She leaned her head back and smiled.)
And loved your beauty with love false or true;
But one man loved the pilgrim soul in you,
And loved the sorrows of your changing face.
  (Now she pointed at Lucy.)

At the Bottom of the Lake

And bending down beside the glowing bars
Murmur, a little sadly, how love fled
    (Victoria's hand fluttered above her lap.)
And paced upon the mountain overhead
And hid his face amid a crowd of stars.

Sam closed the book and lifted his head. He seemed dazed, as though he'd forgotten there were other people present. Victoria sat up in her chair and looked back and forth from Lucy to Sam. Her hand fluttered in the air again. "Do you understand? 'Love fled.' Love flees." Now she looked at her stepdaughter. "That's why you have to grab on and hold tight." She snatched something from the air and shook it in her fist. "Open your eyes, Lucy. This one loves you." She sat back in her chair and smiled. "That's all I wanted to say."

Across the room, Mrs. Hamlin let out a noisy sigh of relief.

"Come on, Vicky," her husband said. She let herself be helped up and led across the room. People moved apart to let them pass and watched through the open door as he delivered her to the bed. She sat down abruptly, as if unaccustomed to the gravity caused by her own weight. He walked back to close the door, and his eyes met Lucy's. His expression was neither embarrassed nor apologetic nor agitated. His face was solemn, and he gently closed the door, turning slowly to the task that awaited him.

People began making excuses to leave: "Rowing back in the dark," and "Mosquitoes will be fierce," and "Got to put some more wood in the stove before the fire goes out." Lucy helped them locate their flashlights, told Mrs. Sweeney not to trouble herself when she started collecting glasses, mechanically thanked everyone as they walked out the door. Mrs. Hamlin paused, touched Lucy's elbow, and told her that she was sorry.

Laden with a tray of half-empty glasses, Sam followed

Lucy into the kitchen. She stood in front of the sink and began filling the dishpan with water. He leaned against the counter and looked at her. When she didn't say anything, he glanced away and then looked back and said, "So what do you think that was all about?"

"I don't know, Sam. She's drunk. Who knows." Lucy squirted soap into the water and picked up a sponge.

"Well, does she do that a lot? Try to impart wisdom to you? Read poems and shit."

She turned to him. He looked angry, as though he suspected Lucy was withholding the piece of information that would make sense of all this. She picked up a glass and began wiping it with the sponge. Feeling his stare still on her, she shrugged.

"It was like she was saying that you're not sure about me."

"That's not what she was saying."

"Then what was the bit about 'Open your eyes, Lucy'?"

"Sam." Lucy threw the sponge into the water. "I don't know what she meant. All I know is she ruined the whole fucking party. And now I have to do all these dishes." She flung her arms out to her sides. "And still make dinner, and I'm tired and I'm pissed off. And if you want to be helpful for a change, you could let this drop and go get the rest of the glasses for me."

"Goddamnit, Lucy," Sam said, walking out. "All I've been is helpful."

Her head sank to her chest. The glass in her hand blurred before her. She began washing and rinsing the glasses and stacking them in the drying rack. Sam walked back into the room.

"I'm not going to let this drop, because this woman, your stepmother, just implied in front of all these people you've known your whole life that you might let me go and you know what—"

With her head still lowered, Lucy tried to focus on the dishes. A trail of tears slid down her nose and dropped into the water.

"I've had to put up with a lot. For weeks, you've been unbelievably tense about this visit. And . . . well, every summer we come up here and you don't even ask me if I want to or not, and I would never even *think* of suggesting we spend our vacation anywhere else only because I know how much this place matters to you. But Christ." Sam placed a handful of glasses on the counter. "I think I have a right to wonder what she meant."

Lucy needed to breathe, but she knew that if she inhaled she would sob. She blinked her eyes, trying to see. He touched her arm, to get her to look at him. She lifted her wet hands to her face, and then slid past him and fled the room.

Lucy ran across the porch and headed down to the dock. The moon, veiled behind clouds, offered little light, and, as she barreled down the path, instinct or habit guided her over the raised, twisted roots without tripping. She reached the edge of the platform; her breath was coming in sobs. She pulled her dress over her head, kicked off her shoes, and dove into the dark water.

As a child, there had never been anyplace to cry here. You could hear the splash of a bass jumping out of the water from across the lake. Sometimes at night, she would slip off to the dock and then slip quietly under the water's surface. She would sit on the lake's bottom and scream warbled, soggy screams, grabbing at the weeds in which she hid herself.

Lucy surfaced and began pulling herself furiously through the water, heading for the center of the lake. She was still crying, but now she was thinking about her father. After this evening, she knew that he wouldn't be coming back. This thought made her stroke even harder. She dove down under the surface and swam toward the bottom. Her eyes were open, but everything was black, and she had no idea of her distance from the shore, no idea of the depth here. She resurfaced to take a breath and then dove again, this time leaving the surface with a strong kick of her legs.

As she plunged for the bottom, she pictured all the things that had been left under the surface of this water, shoes that had fallen out of boats, oarlocks dropped and lost, the fishing pole that had been ripped from her hands. The crib from the old dock built by her grandfather waited, shimmering, just under the surface. Feeling the pressure of her lungs, she kicked as hard as she could and reached her arm out in front of her. And then her hand was skimming weeds; she scooped up a handful of mud and rose toward the surface.

She burst suddenly into the cool night air. Out of breath, she floated on her back, kicking softly to keep herself afloat. The clouds were slipping slowly past the moon, and a slim crescent shone through, casting a pale, tentative light. She stretched her hands to her sides, opening her fingers to let the mud sift out.

Lucy heard a sound she recognized as oars being fitted into locks. She lifted her head and searched the shoreline until she saw a figure pushing off from a dock, her dock. Flipping onto her stomach, she began swimming toward the rowboat. Her arms moved silently through the water. The boat headed out a ways and then drifted for a moment.

When she saw the shadowed figure lengthen upward, she realized it was Sam. Her father knew better than to stand in a rowboat. The water thrashed as the boat careened from side to side. He crouched, shot a hand out to steady himself. When the boat stopped rocking, she saw him begin to rise again.

"Jesus. Don't stand up," she yelled. "Just wait right there."

When she reached the boat, she grabbed the stern. "I guess there's a couple of things I still need to teach you," she said, looking up at him.

Sam looked relieved and smiled. "I'll get it eventually," he said. They headed back to the shore together, she swimming alongside the rowboat, letting the quiet splashings of his oars set her rhythm.

THEY HAD BREAKFAST on the porch so as not to disturb Victoria while she slept it off. Frank Baldwin poured himself another cup of coffee and explained that they would be leaving that morning. "I'll row us to the parking lot and then call Walt from the car to have him tow the boat back."

Lucy nodded, said that sounded fine. "I've been sorting through some stuff, old pictures and letters and things," she said. "You might want something."

"I'll take a look."

"There's also a box of Victoria's old clothes."

"You could probably toss those. They must be pretty old."

"Well, I better ask her."

Sam stood up. "I'm going to make some more coffee. You need anything?"

"Thanks," Lucy said. "I think we're all set."

Lucy's father looked down at his coffee mug, looked out across the water. He took a bite of his eggs, another sip of his coffee, wiped his mouth with his napkin, and then finally met his daughter's eyes. "Look, I'm sorry that it didn't work out. I guess I could have predicted. . . . But, you know," he paused, "maybe I can come back alone sometime."

"Yeah. OK."

Lucy's father touched her arm. "I'm glad to know that you're here, that you'll keep coming here." She looked down, and he put his hand to her chin to raise it. "It's the next best thing," he said.

A LITTLE WHILE LATER, Victoria stepped out on the porch in a bathrobe. "Is there any coffee left?" she asked, shielding her eyes from the bright morning light. She sipped her coffee in the living room while Lucy and her father looked through the papers and pictures she'd put aside for him. He sorted through agendas from past club meetings, old letters, a collection of plans he had drawn for an addition that was never built. Then he turned to the stack of photos. Lucy looked on over his shoulder as he leafed through them. He paused at one of Lucy's mother sitting in the rowboat. She was holding an oar and looked slightly impatient, as if they had somewhere to go and the photo was delaying them. He handed Lucy the pictures and said that she should just keep them here.

Lucy went to fetch the box of Victoria's old clothes. "I don't know if you want any of this stuff," she said, coming back into the room. "I guess they have to be pretty out of style by now." She pulled out a pair of white linen low-slung bell-bottoms. "Otherwise, I'm going to throw everything out."

"I remember those pants," Victoria said, stirring from the couch. "Let me see them." She read the label "Bernard" out loud and hugged the pants to her chest. "That was the most fabulous boutique on Columbus Avenue, back when nobody ever dreamed of shopping on the West Side. It's not around anymore, but he always had the most wonderful dresses, and you could be sure that nobody was going to show up in the same one." She held the pants out to Lucy. "These are back in style. I can't fit into them anymore. Try them on."

Lucy recognized the pattern: now that her stepmother

had gotten her way and they were going to leave, she'd decided to be nice.

"Just try them on," Victoria said. "If you don't want them, then you can throw them away."

For the next half hour, Lucy let her stepmother assemble an outfit from her box of old clothes. They settled on the white linen pants, a black tight-fitted cashmere sweater with abalone buttons up the back, and a brightly colored silk scarf that Victoria produced from her suitcase and draped around Lucy's neck, letting the scarf's ends trail down her back. Victoria led Lucy into the kitchen, where Lucy's father and Sam were cleaning up breakfast. They weren't talking to each other, but they moved around the kitchen in a way that indicated a shared vision had been established.

Victoria pushed Lucy ahead of her and said proudly, "She looks just like I used to, doesn't she? Just like me."

Lucy's father turned and stared at his wife and daughter. Lucy saw a shiver of fright run through his face. "God, you do look alike," he said.

Sam turned and looked also. He smiled and said, "They do, don't they."

Lucy's father kept staring. "Relax, Dad," Lucy said, jutting a leg out to consider the pants. "It's not really my style."

SAM AND LUCY saw Frank Baldwin and Victoria off. The rowboat was crowded with Victoria's luggage. Canvas satchels were piled around her feet. Victoria had dressed up for the journey; a wide floral scarf tied under her chin held a hat in place. Victoria waved to Lucy and Sam, and as Lucy watched them row away in the old wooden boat, they looked to her both regal and unprepared, the gentry fleeing in search of more civilized lands.

Sam gave one last wave and let out a deep sigh. He put an

arm around Lucy's waist, and they turned and headed back to the house. When they reached the porch, Lucy said that she would be just a minute. He hesitated.

"I'm fine." She gave him a light kiss. "I'll be right there."

At the bottom of the porch steps, she paused and then turned away from the water. With her hands in her pockets, she started to walk, slowly, gazing up through the branches, inhaling the last traces of the morning mist. She wandered out to the woods behind the cabin.

When she began coming up here again, she'd gotten to know these woods in a way that she hadn't as a child. She learned about the trees that filled them, all second and third growth, sprung up since the days when this land was used in the lumber trade. She'd been thinking of making a clearing in the valley behind the cabin, taking a few trees down each year to create an open area. It would be decades before it was finished, but she imagined a large clearing where the sun could light up a broad open space. She imagined herself and Sam bringing picnics here and them lying afterward in the sun, full and happy.

Lucy touched various trees, picking out the ones she and Sam would cut down this year, and those skinny birch trees around the edges of her clearing that they'd make room for so they could stretch out their branches. The birch here would not grow in her lifetime to the size of the ones taken by the lumberjack, but she imagined this space a hundred years from now enclosed by huge gentle white limbs.

Loose Talk

PILAR LIFTS her head from her pillow. The silence is thick and constant, and she wonders if the telephone was only ringing in her dreams. Then it rings again, and she slips out of bed, careful not to disturb Max. He doesn't stir, although he could be pretending to be asleep. Pilar feels her way in the dark to the bedroom door and pulls it shut behind her with a soft click.

"Hi."

"Pilar," Andrew says in his low, gravelly voice. "I do like to say your name."

"So say it again," she says, stretching out on the living room couch.

"Pilar," he obliges. "Have you missed me, Pilar?"

In the darkness, Andrew's voice sounds so close, so intimate—Pilar thinks of it traveling along hundreds of miles of trembling wire to arrive so gently against her ear. She makes a sighing sound as if still shaking off sleep and asks him where he is calling from.

"A king-sized bed," he says, "above which hangs one of those ubiquitous," he hisses the last syllable then continues, "beach scenes—you know, an empty chair facing away, toward the ocean. I've seen this same picture in at least a hundred other hotel rooms. The painter should be ashamed of himself."

Pilar recognizes this mood of Andrew's. He doesn't really want to talk; he just needs to hear enough of his own voice to drive the quiet from his room so he can sleep.

"I must be near a coast."

"My coast?" she asks hopefully, although she knows he's not scheduled to play in Boston anytime soon.

His breathing is even and deep. They both listen to it for a while. She suspects he's taken something.

"Your coast, I'm always on," he says finally. "The farthest coast of your mind."

She pulls a pillow into her lap and hugs it. "That's true."

"Sweet Pilar. You make me happy tonight."

Andrew comes to a bit when he tells her about his up-coming tour in Europe: London, Berlin, Prague, and Paris—all the cities where the band will play. He says that he might stay over there for a while, disappear into the French countryside where no one has ever heard of him, but she knows that this is loose talk. She sees Max in the entrance of the living room. She never turned on any lights, and he is a shadow in the doorway. She doesn't say anything, just continues listening to Andrew, and when she looks up again, Max is gone.

"Will you miss me, Pilar?" Andrew asks.

This time she answers. "Yes," she whispers. "I will."

WHEN PILAR opens her eyes, Max is standing by the window, opening the curtains.

"I'm awake," she says. "You can put the light on if you want."

"That's OK." He walks into the bathroom without looking at her.

She watches the door close behind him and turns her head on the pillow. The early morning light washes over the bedroom furniture, making everything look thin and color-less. The limbs of the maple outside the window are dark sil-houettes, like the cutouts of things that might appear outside a person's bedroom window. She imagines for a moment that during the night her apartment slipped its mooring and she has drifted off somewhere. But there's Max in the bathroom—she can hear the water of his shower, she can pic-ture him lathering himself up with soap: face, neck, arms, chest, moving methodically down his body. There's Max on the other side of the closed door, tamping down his anger as he always does until it becomes a hard set to his jaw.

Pilar is to blame for this suffering, yet she observes it with curiosity and slight resentment—resentment because she knows how easily she could rescue Max by simply putting a soothing hand to his cheek, and she chooses not to. She has never mattered so much to someone, and it makes her feel powerful and miserly and scared.

Pilar closes her eyes. I suppose, she thinks, that Andrew's going away is the best thing that could happen. I should get used to not hearing from him, she thinks. I should tell him not to call anymore. *All right, Pilar. Good-bye.* Her fist curls around the quilt as she imagines his indifference.

In the five months Pilar and Max have been living together, Andrew has called four times. The morning after the first call, Pilar told Max that Andrew was a friend and that he liked to touch base with people when he was on the road so he didn't become too isolated. She and Max hadn't even been living together for a month then, and they still regarded each other with cautious acceptance. All Max said was "I didn't know you knew him," as if he wasn't surprised to learn of her friendship with someone whose CDs sat on their shelf. A few weeks later when Andrew called again, Max suggested that the musician should do his touching base at a more reasonable hour.

But Pilar can't tell Andrew when to call her. Each time they say good-bye, she doubts that she'll hear from him again. And for months, she won't, and then one night the phone will ring. She doesn't know why he calls; she doesn't ask. The night Pilar and Andrew met—the only time they have actually seen each other—all they shared was a kiss. Yet it's been going on for almost two years, longer even than she's known Max.

Sometimes when Pilar is home alone she'll spy some evidence of Max, his razor in the medicine cabinet or the cereal he likes in the cupboard, and she'll think, We live together, hoping these words will draw forth some hidden feeling in her and the tide of her affection will finally be loosened.

She glances toward the bathroom. Suddenly, she is desperate to see Max's face—a feeling so strong she can almost taste it.

Max finally emerges with a towel wrapped around his waist. He glances at her and she smiles at him. The corners of his mouth lift warily. She watches him search through a drawer for a pair of matching socks, select a tie and shirt, put on his suit. She would like to ask him to come back to bed for a moment, to lay his body on top of her. She wants to feel his weight above her, his chest rising and falling against her own, to feel how she can't possibly be anywhere but right underneath him. She pulls the quilt up farther and tucks it under her chin. "Let's do something nice tonight," she says to his back. "Go out for dinner or something." He nods vaguely, brushes a pile of change into his palm, deposits it in his trouser pocket, and then he is standing over the bed. He looks at her face for a long moment before he bends down to give her a quick kiss on the forehead. *Wait,* she almost calls as he is heading out the door, but she can't think of what it is she wants to say.

Pilar lies there for a while, then realizes that she's not going to fall back asleep. She sighs and sits up to turn on the light. Today is her only full day off all week from the restaurant where she works as a pastry chef. When Max was still managing the restaurant, he would schedule their days off together, and they would drive to New Hampshire, to the antique markets, or down to Cape Cod if the weather was nice. Now that Max has a real job with the weekends off like normal people, as he says, Pilar is on her own. Without him, though, these trips feel lonely, and she doesn't seem to have friends anymore who can take off for the day at a moment's notice.

She looks down at the quilt covering her, idly tracing her fingers along its zigzagging design. Max's grandmother sent him this quilt when he was in college, the last one she ever made, and Max has joked that he can chart the progress of her senility through its squares. It is true—each one is more fantastically patterned than the last. Pilar smiles, remembering Andrew's response to this story: *Now that's what you call a real crazy quilt.*

On the day that Max moved in, Pilar came home from work and found all of his belongings piled in the living room. A note on the kitchen table said he and his brother had gone out for pizza and beer. She felt like a kid who'd sneaked down early on Christmas morning—she inspected a wicker basket, an elaborate gilded mirror, a wrought-iron plant stand; she sat in the plump upholstered chair. That evening, Pilar learned that many of these things originally belonged to his grandmother. Because he was moving in with a girl-friend, his mother had finally let him have them. "She thinks I'm more settled now," Max explained sheepishly.

"Because you are," Pilar said, reaching out to squeeze his hand.

PILAR HEADS into Cambridge to run a few errands. On her way home, there is hardly any traffic on the roadway and she makes all of the lights. She whizzes past stately homes with their high fences shielding them from the road's din; she zips around the rotaries and past the supermarket, the discount mall, the train station, and finally her own street.

The sun is shining brightly, Pilar has her sunglasses on, and suddenly the day feels full of possibility. Here and there a farm stand appears, nestled in front of a patchwork of fields. Stacks of Christmas trees line their parking lots. The buildings, the split-rail fences, and trees are all crisply edged, their outlines sharpened with air made clear by coldness. But inside the car Pilar is warm. As she speeds down the road, she shuffles through the tape box under her seat for one of Andrew's tapes.

Many times, Pilar has taken to the road with Andrew accompanying her. Before she and Max started dating, when she would leave him behind at the bar and head outside giddy with the knowledge that she was desired, she would crank Andrew's music up loud on her way home, sing along at the top of her voice, and feel a delicious excitement swelling up around her. Then there are the times when she can't imagine a lonelier sound than Andrew's voice, and as she listens, she will find herself touching her fingers to her lips.

Pilar imagines him now, en route to Fort Lauderdale, lying on his bed on the tour bus. She wonders if he is thinking of her, too. She knows that he does sometimes think of her. He has told her that he imagines what he would do if they met again, the ways that he would love her. When Andrew relates these things in the quiet, rhythmic voice he uses for this kind of talk, Pilar stays very still, her only movement her hands as they keep company to his words. And when he's finished, it is her turn.

Sometimes he'll tell Pilar that she is special, and his words will tap some ancient feeling in her—the feeling, when she was young, of running after a ball, drunk with her own speed, or offering some observation to her parents that struck astonishment into their faces, and she will wonder how she ever forgot these moments.

The tape ends and Pilar turns the radio off. She's been driving for close to an hour, turning left and right indiscriminately, and she realizes that she doesn't know where she is.

She stops at a gas station and calls Max at work. As she waits for him to finish with another call, she stares out at the empty road. By the time he picks up, she's shivering.

"What's up?" he says. "Where are you?"

"Somewhere off Route Two. I don't know exactly."

"Well," Max says and pauses. "Well," he says again. "Did you call for something in particular, because it's kind of busy here."

"No," she says and thinks to herself, Nothing in particular. An intimate tone of voice, some common reference— anything would have been enough to draw the world closed so it's just the two of them.

"I just called to say hi, I guess," she says.

An automated voice comes on the line to demand twenty-five cents more. Pilar can hear Max trying to talk through the recording. "Listen, I've got to go," he says. "But I'll see you at home, OK."

Pilar hangs up the phone, thrusts her hands into her jacket pockets, and leans against her car. She notices the gas station attendant watching her through the storefront window. She stares back at him, feeling close to tears. She glances away and looks through her purse, as though searching for change. You can't stand here forever, she tells herself. But picturing the apartment now, filled with her and Max's things and all the photos of them—on beaches, at parties, huddled with a group of their friends—she cannot bring herself to go home.

She fishes in her pocket for more change. She knows that Andrew's band usually stays in Hilton hotels; she tries three in the Fort Lauderdale area before she finds one where an A. Feiner is expected. Each time Pilar hears the helpful voice saying "Hilton?" her conviction that calling Andrew is the right thing to do strengthens. She leaves a message for him to phone her back tonight. She says it's important.

WITH DIRECTIONS from the attendant, the drive back is quick. Pilar rides in silence; her mind is blissfully empty. She bustles around the rest of the afternoon, cleaning the apartment and doing the laundry. On her way into the kitchen for a glass of water, she stops in the living room and looks around. The baroque music she put on earlier is still playing, the cushions of the couch are plumped, the colors of the upholstered chair bright in the afternoon sun, and she thinks how it really isn't that hard to be happy.

She's in the bath when the phone rings. It's Max, wondering if she made it home all right.

"I'm sorry I couldn't talk. The phone was ringing like crazy. I don't know why people get inspired on Friday afternoon to try to wrap things up. And then Carl, you know the one who might be moving to the New York office—"

Max goes on to tell her about a possible job opening on the trading desk, how although he's only been there for a short while he thinks he might have a good shot at it.

Pilar's head rests on a towel folded over the lip of the tub. Her eyes are closed, and her face is raised as though offering it up to the sun. "That sounds great," she says. Max is what her mother would call a real go-getter. Even at the restaurant, where everyone takes pride in doing their jobs with as little effort as possible, Max developed schemes to improve business, theme nights and frequent-diner cards.

She starts to ask when he's coming home, but Max interrupts and puts her on hold. She adds more hot water to the bath, which is beginning to cool.

"So," he says when he returns, "there's a party tonight. A guy here and his wife just moved into a new place in the South End, and—"

"You want to go?"

"Well, yeah, kind of. It's supposed to be a really nice place. A town house on one of those cul-de-sacs."

"I guess," she says.

"You don't have to," Max says. "I could just stop by alone."

With more conviction, she says, "No, we should go. It's about time I met some of your friends from work."

After she hangs up, the idea of a party begins to seem more appealing. Since she and Max moved in together, they have hardly ever gone to parties or out to bars. She likes the thought of getting dressed up and being introduced to Max's work friends; she has an idea of what they're like— conventional and benign. It's been a while since she stood out in a crowd.

She notices that the nail polish she put on a few days ago has begun to chip. After her bath, she can fix her nails, do her makeup and hair, and decide what to wear for the party. At this rate, the rest of the afternoon will pass in no time. Then Max will be back, they'll grab a bite in town, and there'll only be the party to get through before she can return home and sleep until Andrew's call awakens her.

Her fingers beat a rhythm on the tub's edge. She lets the water drain out and scrubs every inch of her skin with a loofah. She applies a clay mask to tighten the pores of her face and then puts on full makeup. In the middle of applying her mascara, she pulls back from the mirror for a moment. Dropping her chin, turning her face slightly to one side, she looks up at herself and smiles shyly. A large, loose happiness buzzes in the air. She strokes more mascara on her lashes, now humming to herself under her breath. She arranges her blond curls on top of her head in a complicated pile.

WHEN PILAR comes into the kitchen dressed for the party, Max is standing in front of the refrigerator. One foot is crossed over the other, resting on the ball of his toe; his arm drapes along the top of the open door as he peers inside. He is Tuesday's child, Pilar has told him, full of grace. She walks over and brushes her lips against the fine hairs of his neck. He startles and takes a few steps backward. His expression, when he turns around and regards her outfit, remains neutral. She is wearing a black silk blouse, sheer, her bra visible underneath.

Pilar looks down at the skin swelling above the cups of her bra. "Is it too much?" She lifts her breasts in her hands and looks up at him, grinning.

Max snorts incredulously and says, "You'll certainly be noticed." But his tone of voice makes it clear what he thinks about this kind of attention.

Pilar follows him to the hall closet.

"You're not going to be warm enough," Max says when he sees the jacket that Pilar selects.

She zips up her leather jacket and says that she'll be fine. Max sighs and selects a scarf from the hook by the door and wraps it around her neck.

"You're the one who helped me pick this jacket out. Remember? It's supposed to be warm enough for me to ride on the back of your motorcycle."

"My motorcycle." He raises his eyebrows.

Pilar punches him lightly on the arm. "You were never really going to buy a motorcycle. You were just trying to make me fall in love with you."

He smiles and opens the door for her to walk out. "I guess I was," he says, but his expression changes as he answers, as though he's forgotten why he is smiling.

Pilar is still not accustomed to the evening getting dark so early. There are no street lamps on the dead-end street where they live, but many of the houses they pass are already bright with Christmas lights. Outlines of porch railings and trees blink in the darkness.

Pilar links her arm through Max's. "You were right. It is cold," she says, putting her other hand into her jacket pocket.

"It's definitely winter," Max says, blowing a plume of breath in front of him.

Pilar looks toward the lighted houses. "Hey, we should get our tree soon." Among the things Max inherited from his grandmother is a collection of Christmas ornaments.

"I thought you didn't like Christmas," Max says.

"I do so. Why would you say that?"

He pauses in his step slightly. "Um, because you made fun of me for trying to get people to sing carols last year at the restaurant's Christmas party."

Beside her, she can hear his breath rising and falling evenly in his throat. She wishes she could reach back through time and shake that girl by the shoulders.

On the subway ride into town, Pilar asks questions about Max's friends from work, and as he answers, they get to laughing about how well she knows their lives, even though she has never met them.

MAX FETCHES some drinks, and they stand in one corner of the living room, surveying the party. Pilar watches another couple across the room: the woman stands a step behind the man's shoulder; she swirls the ice cubes of her drink as he tells the man beside him a story, flicking the man's chest with the back of his hand as he talks. Reed Swallens, Pilar decides, the fellow who is having an affair with his assistant and thinks no one knows.

Pilar notices an athletic-looking blond girl wearing tight black pants and a gray blazer and, what first gets Pilar's attention, a pair of high-heeled black lace-up boots. She can't place her among the women Max has told her about. Despite the boots, the blonde's sex appeal is more cheerful than threatening. She keeps glancing toward the corner of the room where Max and Pilar stand. Pilar nods over to her. "Who's that?"

"Oh, that's Barbara. She's new."

"Aha." Pilar regards her. "She's attractive."

"She's nice. I'll introduce you."

As if on cue, Barbara begins heading over to them. "Well, if it isn't Maxwell Richard?" she says, placing the stress in his last name on the first syllable and giving it a long *e* the way Max's French ancestors would have said it. Pilar catches Max's eye and raises her eyebrows at this foreign pronunciation. Barbara continues, "Is this the lovely lady I've heard so much about?" She laughs in a way that makes Pilar wonder what Barbara has heard.

"I'm Barbara Marks," she says, offering a serious handshake.

"So," Pilar begins when it becomes clear that Max can't think of anything to say, "Max tells me you've just started up."

"I guess it's two months now, but it feels like I've been

here forever already. Everybody's been really nice." Barbara shines her smile on Max.

"Are you from the Boston area originally?" Pilar asks.

"God no. I hope I don't sound like I am." Barbara goes on to tell them about how she was a navy brat growing up and all the different places her daddy was stationed. She swings her ponytailed head back and forth from Pilar to Max as she talks. But, Barbara says, jabbing her finger in the air to call attention to her big finish, for the last seven years she had the distinct pleasure of living in Florida, a place that no one in their right mind would leave willingly. At the mention of Florida, a quiet thrill runs through Pilar's stomach, and she says, "Then why did you leave?"

Barbara glances at Max as though she is uncertain she made herself clear. "To take the job, of course."

Pilar realizes from this look and the slight adjustment of Barbara's head to set it more proudly on her neck that she, Barbara, has a very good position with the firm, the kind that no one in their right mind would turn down. So she's one of those, Pilar thinks. She has known women like her before, in gym classes in high school, women who pick up a field-hockey stick for the first time and take off down the field, never doubting that they will know how to use it. Pilar looks down at her drink, thinking absently how Barbara must make a lot of money, much more than Max, and how that might really impress him. She finishes off the last sip and tilts her glass toward Max.

"You need another drink. Is that a wine spritzer?" Barbara peers into Pilar's empty glass.

"Vodka tonic," Max answers.

"Oh, the hard stuff. You're a party girl, huh?" She winks at Pilar. "I like that. Well, I was just heading off to the kitchen to get another drink myself. One vodka tonic coming right up."

"No. Don't bother," Pilar starts to say, but Barbara cuts her off. "I won't be a minute. You two stay right here."

After she walks away, Pilar turns to Max. "Maxwell Richard?" She imitates Barbara's pronunciation.

"That's the way it's supposed to be said."

"You told her to say it that way?"

"I told everyone in the office. It's how you are supposed to say it." Max isn't looking at her. He taps his fingers against the edge of his beer bottle and glances around the room.

Pilar takes a deep breath. "Well, you're right. She is nice. Good-natured. Very positive, if maybe a little," Max turns to her and she can't resist, "banal," she finishes in her best French accent.

"Well," he says harshly, "there's nothing wrong with try-ing to be decent."

The ugliness in his voice makes Pilar cringe. She has never heard him talk like this before. You did that to him, she thinks.

"I've got to pee," she says finally.

"All right," Max says. He nods toward a guy standing nearby and starts to head over to him.

Since Pilar doesn't really need to use the bathroom, she stands in the hallway next to it, outside the door. People walk by, nodding hello, but no one stops to talk to her except one girl who asks if she's in line. Pilar can see into the living room. Max is joined by Barbara, who hands over the vodka tonic. Pilar waits for Max to glance around, over Barbara's shoulder, to look for her. But he doesn't. He is laughing at something Barbara is saying. He puts down his empty beer and reaches out to touch her arm. He leans his laughing face into her. He straightens up and takes a sip of Pilar's drink.

She slips into the bathroom. She stands in front of the mirror. With all the makeup on, she doesn't even look like herself. Max once asked her why she wore so much makeup when they went out, and she told him that she didn't want to share her face with just anybody. He shook his head and walked out of the bathroom, calling over his shoulder that she was crazy. He lived with a crazy woman.

Someone knocks on the bathroom door. Pilar glances in the mirror and sees that tears have made her mascara run. She leans down to flush the toilet and over the whoosh of water calls that she'll be right out. She left her purse in the entryway when they came in, so she can't even fix herself up. After she washes her face, her features look small and fragile. Her eyelids are swollen slightly and pink.

Max calls through the door. "Pilar, are you OK?"

"I'll be right out."

He stands in the entrance, blocking her way. "What's wrong. Were you crying?"

"My makeup was bothering my eyes so I washed my face."

"I was looking for you. Where did you go?"

"Just chatting. Making party chatter, you know." Pilar turns to the living room and sees that Barbara and another man are watching this exchange.

"Do you want to leave?"

She glances at a couple in the hallway; they are leaning against a wall, their heads bent close, as though there were no one else around. The man raises one hand and adjusts the collar of the woman's blouse. She stands completely still while he touches her, and when he removes his hand, she laughs lightly and runs her fingers through her hair.

"Pilar, do you want to go?"

"Why don't you stay, Max. I can take a cab. These are your friends. You should stay."

Max studies her face.

"Will you just call me a cab?" Pilar makes her voice light.

She feels as though she's trying to hold up something unbearably heavy and as long as she can maintain this buoyant tone she can keep this heavy thing from falling.

"Sure," he says finally, sounding grateful. "Right away," he adds.

"I'll be over there." She waves vaguely behind her. Her voice has risen up another octave, nearing the pitch of hysteria.

Pilar starts down the hallway toward the front door, and Max heads in the other direction to the kitchen. She pauses next to the couple, leans into them slightly for a moment, thinking that if they would include her, if the man brushed the side of her cheek with his hand, then she would be able to stay at this party, she'd be able to talk in a reasonable pitch; she could lean against this wall with them and rock back and forth with quiet laughter. She walks past them and then slowly across the living room, placing her feet carefully. She feels everyone's gaze upon her.

Outside, Pilar watches the party through the living room's bay window as she waits for her cab. Max is out of sight, and Barbara is talking to a plain-looking woman seated on the couch. Barbara's profile is to the window. She keeps leaning down, stretching over from her hips so her blazer pulls up to expose her ass clamped into her tight pants. The dowdy woman's face lights up every time Barbara addresses her. Pilar guesses that the woman is the receptionist or a secretary and is grateful enough for Barbara's attention to pretend that this important jobholder always talks to her like this.

Pilar can hear music through a window cracked despite the cold, some upbeat generic jazz. Andrew would hate this, she thinks. She watches Barbara glance around the room, raising her drink to sip through the small straw, pursing her mouth, her eyes wide, taking everything in. She stands with one hand on her hip, pulsing slightly to the beat.

In a little while, Pilar will be home. She'll go right to bed,

and she'll be sleeping when Andrew calls. At the urgent ringing of the phone, she will bolt up, breathing hard, and see
that Max isn't there beside her. Before she can decide how to
explain to Andrew what is happening in her life, between
her and Max, Andrew will say that he knows why she called
him.

"Is this what you want, Pilar? To talk? You like to talk,
don't you."

But right now, standing outside the party, the air cold and
close, drawing all her awareness tight against herself, Pilar
closes her eyes. If she concentrates, she can still remember
the feeling she had that night when she met Andrew. She
stood right in front of the stage, and as Andrew turned
toward the drummer for a solo, his gaze scanned the crowd,
and Pilar caught his eye and grinned. Andrew smiled back,
looking a little grateful beneath his serious coolness, and she
felt that she had cracked him a bit and slipped inside. Then
she closed her eyes so she could hold his gaze in her mind
and she was standing alone in a room with him. She moved
with him, following his voice, the rhythms he played on his
guitar, and she felt that he was following her, too, letting the
way she moved lead him through the song. The other musicians dropped away until it was just Andrew's voice and the
melody he was searching out on the strings, moving carefully now, aware that, together, he and Pilar were traveling to
a place they'd never been before.

The Trouble with Mr. Leopold

Mr. Leopold had once worked as an image consultant, and every year, for one day, he met with the girls from the junior class to consult with us about our images. Woodbridge Country Day had only been coeducational for four years; no one thought to question why just the girls were offered this opportunity, and every girl signed up.

While I sat on the wooden chair outside his office waiting for my turn, I tried to make sense of the Emily Dickinson poem which had been assigned as homework for my American literature class: "My Life had stood—a Loaded Gun— / In Corners—till a Day / The Owner passed—identified— / And carried Me away—." I looked up from the book, sighed, and lowered my head once more. The truth was that I was scared of Mr. Leopold.

The office door opened, and Jane, my best friend, walked, or rather sauntered, out, the blazer we were required to wear as part of our school uniform off. It dangled from one finger down her back. "N-n-next," she drawled.

I stood up and peered inside. Mr. Leopold sat on a couch

under the bank of windows at the far side of the room. There were no lights on, and his small dark figure was hard to distinguish from the brown couch. He was short, with stumpy legs and a long torso, and hairy—a mass of black hair spilled back from his forehead, he wore a full thick beard, and a shadowy tangle peeked above the knot of his tie.

"Hello, Celia. Come in. Come in," he said, peering back at me from under his dark beetle brows. "Close the door, please. Walk toward me. Yes. That's right."

As I moved across the room, I became conscious of his gaze on my legs and suddenly found myself lurching toward him. When I had covered half the distance between us, he told me to stop. "Show me your knees," he said.

I looked blankly down at my legs. I had no opinion of my knees; no idea whether they were attractive or the ugliest pair on earth. Why did he want to look at them? If he had told me to turn around and wiggle my hips, I would have been less surprised, but this interest in my knees carried with it a whiff of perversion. I squinted, trying to picture them hidden under the cover of my skirt, and then there they were in my mind's eye—I saw how they jutted out insistently from my thin legs, how their skin, delicately puckered, was reminiscent of other intimate folds of flesh. My face grew hot.

"Your knees. Your knees," Mr. Leopold repeated impatiently. "Lift up your skirt so I can see them."

Slowly I raised the bottom of my kilt to the crest of my kneecaps, and Mr. Leopold nodded thoughtfully. "Yes, all right. You may wear patterned stockings. Not all women can. But *you* may. In fact, patterned stockings would do you a great deal of good, accentuate the curve of your legs more. They're a bit too thin actually."

"Patterned stockings?"

"Yes. As opposed to sheer or opaque tights. You should

definitely avoid opaque, unless you want your legs to look like a little bird's poking out from underneath your skirt. By patterned, I mean, of course, something with a little texture, a rib or net, something along those lines."

"OK," I said dubiously. Net stockings. As in fishnet stockings. I had an idea of the kind of woman who wore such things.

"Now I'd like you to smile," he said.

I aimed my smile over his head, out his office window. A group of little girls was chasing a boy across the front lawn. One girl caught up with the boy and flung him to the ground. I felt the rest of my face join my mouth in smiling.

"Hmm. Yes. I've noticed this about you before. Your smile. It's lopsided. One side of your mouth rises up higher than the other. It makes you look . . . ," Mr. Leopold paused, "a little slow, which I know you're not, and distrusting too, and that is not desirable."

I was still clutching my kilt in my hands, rubbing the rough polyester fabric between my fingertips. Mr. Leopold's own mouth inched up into a stingy smile. I let go of my skirt.

He rose to his feet, circled me once, then came to rest at my side. I kept my eyes trained forward. A whooshing sound rose up out of the quiet, like the rush of wind past my ear, as though I were sailing out over a ravine on a swing with Leopold behind me, pushing. Then the sound of air reversing. His breath was moving wetly through his mouth.

"Stand up straighter," he said finally.

Immediately, I straightened my back. My posture was a small, private pride of mine. I didn't try to hide my breasts like some girls did, slumping forward in embarrassment.

"More!"

I glanced at him out of the corner of my eye. He had unbuttoned his suit jacket, and his chest jutted out between the flared lapels. I arched my spine slightly.

"That's better," he said. "There's no need to be ashamed."

He moved around to face me and took a step forward so our heads were no more than a foot apart. I was trying not to breathe, not to let anything from my body touch him. I could see the minute shifts in his expression as he decided what to do with me. Arrogance, desire, disgust, and pity all flickered past.

He inclined his head forward another few degrees and the wetness of his breath filled the small space between us. In a whisper, he said, "You should stand closer to people. Get in their personal space a little more. Don't be so afraid to be noticed."

Then he straightened up, buttoned his jacket, and took his seat. A slackening passed down through my body, as though just now my muscles and organs were coming under the effects of gravity. I breathed a quiet sigh of relief. Mr. Leopold was still breathing heavily, although he had resumed his relaxed pose. He asked if I had any questions. All I could think to do was to pretend that I was Jane, which was something I sometimes did in moments requiring nerve and courage. I let a wry smile lift one side of my mouth, put a hand on my hip, and told him with as much irony in my voice as I dared that I thought he had made everything perfectly clear. I thanked him for his time.

"My pleasure," he said. "Please send the next girl in."

I stepped into the hall, into the din and blur of a stream of students. Past the blue blazers, the glen-plaid kilts, was Jane leaning up against the wall. I glanced down and saw that my shirttail was pulled out of my skirt. Quickly, I tucked it back in. I buttoned my blazer, shifted my backpack on my back. I felt as though I were missing something, that I had left something behind in Leopold's room, but I couldn't think what it would be. Jane caught my eye and waved me over.

"About time," she said. "What the hell were you doing in there?"

Her question slapped shame across my face, and my cheeks reddened. *The same thing you were,* I started to say, but she was already heading off down the hallway. "Well, apparently I am just too much for Mr. Leopold's tastes." Her voice was sly and pleased. "I wear too much makeup, talk too loud and too much, have too much upper-body motion when I walk, whatever the hell that means, and I should never, ever, wear patterned stockings. My legs are plenty curvy already. So Cee-Cee, you know what I told him?" She turned to me, shaking her collection of silver bangles down her raised arm. "That I thought I was just right the way I was, and plenty of people, plenty of guys, agreed with me. I told him that. Right to his face. And then, listen to this, I told him that I thought this school was full of shit. Well, I didn't say 'shit,' actually, I said 'crap,' but same difference. I told him that they act like they want us to be these ambitious, intelligent young women, and then they treat us like this is a finishing school, and the only reason to go to a good college is to find a husband who will make enough money to pay the country club dues so we can lead the same exact boring life as our parents. So." She took a deep breath and turned to me. "What's wrong with you?"

"Oh," I said, startled. I had been trying to picture myself telling off Mr. Leopold, an option which hadn't occurred to me. Maybe he was right. Maybe I was afraid to make myself noticed. "Um. He said I can wear patterned stockings—"

"Well, lucky you," interrupted Jane. "God forbid you should suffer through life in plain old panty hose. Or worse, pants!"

"Do you want to know or not?"

"All right. What else?" She had stopped walking and faced

me, her eyebrows arched, her hands on her hips, her indignation temporarily, tenuously, reeled in.

"He said . . ." Jane shifted her weight from one foot to another. "Well, he said that I should stand closer to people."

I STOOD at the window of Mr. Leopold's classroom, watching the mothers. Every other Wednesday afternoon they arrived, armed with pruning shears and kneeling stools, to maintain the school's formal garden. In the old pictures of the garden in the front hall, the holly and boxwood were shaped into soaring turrets and figures of fantastic birds, but after years of pruning by the volunteer mothers, most of the topiary was no longer recognizable. Leaning spires jutted up intermittently from the hedge's top. At the ends of rows where birds once perched, ominous lopsided shapes rose out of the shrubbery like waves about to crash down upon the walkway. Very few of the mothers knew what they were doing. At their own homes, gardeners took care of the pruning.

The mothers sank to their knees, one after another, as though some invisible prophet were passing by atop the hedge before them. They lifted their shears and haphazardly began to cut the branches. I scanned the backs of these women, knowing that I wouldn't find my mother's crisp cotton shirt among the collection. She was excused from the gardening duty since she worked long late hours in the city as an editor for a cooking magazine.

My father, who made his living as a writer and worked at home, was occasionally pressed into service—to address literature classes or judge poetry contests or read the manuscripts of one or two young English teachers who were aspiring writers. He liked Woodbridge Country Day; he liked the ivy-covered stones of its gated entrance, its apple orchards and formal gardens; he even liked the exorbitant tuition. For a man who went to public school in Brooklyn and then City College, he looked more at home strolling along the oak-paneled hallways in his sports jacket and blue jeans than most of the students. His appearances here, especially if I wasn't expecting him, always made me uneasy, as though I were the one who didn't belong.

Mr. Leopold sought out my father during these visits. He'd also been a Brooklyn boy, a point which he mentioned repeatedly, as though this fact should establish some feeling of camaraderie between the two men. Anyone could see that they weren't alike in the least. My father was handsome, charming, a success. Mr. Leopold was, well, Mr. Leopold. Whenever he chatted with my father, he would pepper his speech with obscure literary references. My dad lobbed them right back, with an extra bit of polish—the next line of the poem, perhaps, or a reference to a superior translation. "Right. Of course," Mr. Leopold would sputter, his eyes blinking rapidly as he committed this information to memory for their next meeting. If I told my dad about Mr. Leopold's analysis of me, he would make quick work of it, all right, repeating the teacher's words until they became foolish, until I felt like a fool for ever believing them.

I looked past the formal gardens across the great expanse of frequently resodded lawn. At the far end stood a high stone fence, beyond which lay the Long Island Sound. I watched two boys as they nimbly scaled this fence and dropped down to the other side. In my mind, I followed them across the beach to a spot behind one of the cement bulwarks separating the properties of the mansions perched along this stretch of coastline. Crouched there, out of sight and away from the wind, they would light their cigarettes or perhaps a joint that would be hastily passed between them. I laid my hand against the wavy pane of the old glass, feeling the heat of the afternoon sun. If the window were open, I might have caught the briny scent of the damp sea air, carried off the water on a warm gust of wind.

When I heard Mr. Leopold's voice, I turned to take my seat, but suddenly he was at my side, glancing down at the mothers. "They really butcher those poor shrubs, don't they?" he said. His tone was conspiratorial, as though in his office that morning we had arrived at some agreement.

"They're volunteers," I answered incongruously.

"So of course one can't complain," he said. "Well, a little bit of pruning can be helpful now and then." He cocked his head back and observed me with an artist's squinted eye. "Trim up those rough edges, you know."

I ducked away, glancing at the wall clock behind him, and said, "Isn't class supposed to start?"

Presently, Mr. Leopold began his lecture on the history of the American cinema. *You've heard, no doubt, of the magic lantern. . . .* No one was listening, especially not the girls. Courtney Jameson, in front of me, had her leg stretched out into the aisle. She rotated the limb one way, then the other, tensing and relaxing her calf muscle, and admiring its gentle slope. Next to me, Jane was drawing a caricature of Mr. Leopold, making his legs even more stumpy, his torso longer; hair covered his face, came out of his ears, sprouted all over his chest in dense dark squiggles. I kept smiling down into my notebook, trying to feel which side of my mouth raised up higher than the other.

As Mr. Leopold proceeded from silent movies to talkies, Charlie Chaplin, *Citizen Kane,* his gaze raked across the sea of students in search of someone to meet his eye. Eventually he gave up and focused on a high spot along the back wall. I glanced at Jane. Every few minutes, she would tilt her portrait in my direction. "That's great," I kept whispering, my head lowered toward hers, each time trying to sound more enthusiastic than the last. I had never gotten around to telling her the rest of what Mr. Leopold had said to me. Repeating his criticisms in my mind, I could hear how silly they sounded, but something—remembering the trespass of his gaze upon me, or the embarrassment of discovering these things about myself, things I hadn't realized before—was making my throat tight.

Finally Mr. Leopold announced that we were ready to watch a film. He dimmed the overhead lights, and I was alone with my crooked smile, my bad posture and spindly legs, my fear of being noticed. "Be sure to pay close attention," Mr. Leopold was saying. "What I'd like you to do . . ." I was reminded of the first time I saw myself on videotape— dancing at a cousin's wedding. I fancied that I was a good dancer, rhythmic and cool, but when the camera swept around to light on me for a moment, I saw how ridiculous I looked, pounding my fists through the air in time to the music, like someone throwing a temper tantrum. And now I had yet another image of myself to mock my errant hope that I was not ridiculous, that I was just fine the way I was. "—a review of the film," Mr. Leopold's voice continued.

I leaned over to Jane and whispered, "What'd he say?"

"We have to write a review for homework," she whispered back. "You know, did you like it and why."

I knew what a review was. My dad wrote them some-times, and I'd heard from him, more than once, that not just anyone could write them. Great, I thought. Just great.

AT NINE-THIRTY that evening I went looking for my father. I found him in his study, reclined in his easy chair, a book in his lap. We chatted for a moment about my cat, who was plucking at the Oriental rug in the living room again. Finally,

I told him I had to write a paper. He glanced at his watch and gave me a disapproving look. Then he sighed, tucked the jacket flap over the page he was reading, and closed his book.

"And you're having trouble," he said.

Paralysis was more like it. I'd been sitting in my room for the last hour and a half, starting lines only to scratch them out, standing up, then sitting down, berating myself to think, think, think. But for every idea that I'd come up with, I could make an argument against it. No point had seemed irrefutable. Finally, I'd stood up and studied my face in the mirror; I threw my shoulders back and smiled, the most even, the most symmetrical smile I could summon.

My father was waiting for an answer. I shrugged and banged the heel of my shoe against the doorjamb.

"Celia, stop that," he said.

He tossed his book on a table and raised the chair to an upright position. "What's the subject?"

"It's supposed to be a review—"

"A review," he repeated with pleased surprise.

"Yeah. Of this film, *Occurrence at Owl Creek Bridge*." I was sitting in his desk chair at this point, unbending and bending a paper clip. I looked up to see him raise his eyebrows at the name of the film.

"It's based on some famous short story by Ambrose Bierce."

"It can't be too famous. I've never heard of it."

"It's old, you know, not . . ."

"Contemporary?"

"Right."

I riffled the cluster of pencils standing in a crockery jug.

"Will you please stop fidgeting with everything. I just sharpened those." When my father had trouble writing, he sharpened and resharpened his pencils.

I placed my hands in my lap. He rubbed a palm over one eye.

"Did you like the film?"

"No." That was as far as I'd gotten in my room.

"Just state your opinion and then give a short summary of the film and your reasons for not liking it."

"Right. Sure."

"Why didn't you like it?"

"It was stupid." I knew that wasn't good enough. "Manipulative," I added hesitantly.

"A poet once said that the truest poetry was the most feigning. Manipulation is not necessarily grounds for thinking something is stupid. Was the manipulation—"

"Easy," I said. "It was an easy manipulation." I explained how the surprise of the film's beginning, that the rope to hang a young soldier miraculously breaks so he can escape and return to his wife and daughter, turns out to be a dream. I explained that the whole movie, his dodging from a volley of shots and cannonballs, his flight through the woods, the scene where he's running toward his wife's open arms, is just a fantasy. "I mean, that's so easy." I raised my arms in disgust. "And it's unfair to spend a whole movie tricking you into believing that this guy is so lucky that he actually escaped and then, boom, he's dangling at the end of a rope."

"Why do you think Bierce makes it all a fantasy?"

"Well . . ." *That* question hadn't occurred to me, actually. My hand strayed across the desk toward the stapler. Gently, I pushed down on it until the hinge squeaked. "Sorry," I said, curling my fingers back. "Well," I began again. "Just as the guy is about to be hung, he closes his eyes and pictures his wife and kid, and they're, like, angelic, you know. They're both beautiful and they're kind of glowing in this pale light, and so the whole escape is kind of about how the purity, the force of this love, can beat death. So obviously, this guy, Ambrose, doesn't believe that love can do that."

My father sighed and said, "The rather tired notion of death triumphing over romantic love."

After my father and I talked, I hurried back to my room with a topic sentence and a few one-liners. But somehow, during those twenty paces between his study and my desk, any clarity I had faded, and when I sat down to write, though I kept repeating his phrases to myself, their meanings remained hovering, incandescent, above me, only casting a brighter light on my confusion.

Twice, I went back to his room. Twice, he reviewed what I had written and showed me where I'd lost my argument. I looked over his shoulder, my eyes growing tired and heavy, and tried to make sense of what he was saying. I knew that he was right, but I didn't quite see *how* he was right. "Celia, you're not concentrating," he admonished. "You're never going to get anywhere in life if you don't learn how to concentrate." It was true. I wasn't paying attention. My mind was too busy condemning me to a life replete with failures of which this paper was just the beginning. I couldn't do anything right. I would never be able to do anything right. Where were the other kids in my class at this moment? Surely not harassing their fathers who were seconds away from throwing up their hands in despair.

Once more, he shored me up with a few ready-made sentences and sent me back to my room. By this time, the focus of my paper had been elevated into a general discussion of successful and unsuccessful uses of manipulation in literature and film with a few references to Edgar Allan Poe and Hawthorne thrown in for good measure. I read and reread these sentences, trying to distill their meaning, but each word seemed more important than the last, and before I'd even arrived at the end of a line, my brain was overcrowded with all these words claiming their preeminence. In a desperate rush, I wrote out a few paragraphs on which I hung these weighty assertions. Then I skimmed over the new draft. I couldn't make heads or tails of it, but I was calmed momentarily by the thought that perhaps this was a good sign.

The third time back in my father's study, I was in the middle of reading my revised opening aloud when he snatched the paper from me, saying that no child of his was going to turn in this piece of garbage. He crumpled my pages into a ball. It was almost eleven-thirty, and I began to cry. "I can't do it," I said, sobbing loudly. "I just can't write it."

He shut his book with a snap. "Jesus, Celia. It's not the end of the world."

"I hate Mr. Leopold," I said, lowering my head into my hands.

"This is for him? *That* pompous fool. Why didn't you say so?"

"Can you just help me, please?"

My father sighed and tilted up his easy chair. He got up and moved over to his desk, a pointed finger pinning me to a spot behind his shoulder. "Stay there," he said. "Stay right there."

My mother appeared, the pitch of my desperation having reached my parents' bedroom, where she'd been reading a cookbook. The scene in my father's study was not unfamiliar. I had often gone to him for help on a school paper, though always in the past I had managed to eventually produce something that could meet his approval. She stood in the doorway, her hands invisible, tucked into the sleeves of her white terry-cloth bathrobe, like a monk. "Is there anything I can do?" she asked cautiously.

I turned my teary face toward her, wishing that she would come to me; that her hands would emerge to steer me by my shoulders to bed; that she would murmur a promise about a sick note, an assurance that the paper could be written tomorrow; that everything would be fine in the morning.

"Leave us alone." An arm shot up from behind my father's desk.

She hesitated, and then her hands finally appeared. She clutched the doorknob and said, "Well, I'll close the door then." A shake of her head for me that meant, *You should know better than to ask him for help,* and she was gone.

I turned back to my father, who was furiously writing, his pencil point making small, angry scratching noises.

"Bierce. *E-a* or *i-e*?"

My breath sputtered in my chest. "Like 'fierce,'" I managed. He looked up, concern briefly clouding the concentration in his gaze, and said, "Why don't you sit down?"

After he finished the first page, he sent me to my room to copy it over. Some of the words he used I didn't know— "transcendence" and "denouement." Since his handwriting was hard to read, I had to look them up to check their spelling. I did convince him to take out the comparison to "The Metamorphosis," since we weren't reading Kafka until senior year. It was after one when I finally got into bed. I fell asleep to the low grumble of my parents' bickering. The pitch of my mother's voice rose and became indignant, and I knew that she was trying to defend me.

MR. LEOPOLD returned the papers the following week. His sinister smile when passing back mine made my heart knock against my chest. For the duration of the class, I left the pages lying facedown on my desk. The moment the bell rang, I was out the door, racing down to the girls' locker room. Finished, I thought. Kaput! My life of failure had begun. My mind did entertain one dim hope: If I was out, wouldn't they have told me by now? In the furthermost shower stall, perched on a bench, I flipped the paper over to see written in Mr. Leopold's red pen: *C-plus.* A C-plus! I could have done that without my dad's help! I read on: *The best negative review I received, although this film doesn't deserve such a panning. Also, you broke the golden rule of review writing—never reveal a surprise ending!* I began to laugh, a hearty, deep-bellied laugh that echoed back to me off the locker room's tiled floor and walls.

Two WEEKS later my father was driving the afternoon car-pool home from school when Jane, in the backseat, began imitating Mr. Leopold. He had a habit in class of slipping off his loafers and tucking one foot underneath his behind. Per-haps he recognized that he appeared rather diminutive seated at the large table, and so he was attempting to prop himself up more in his seat. Sometimes when he was warm-ing up to his subject, he would begin to rock back and forth on top of his foot.

Jane kept squirming and laughing and bouncing and demanding that we guess who she was. "Come on, this is easy," she said.

"What are you doing back there?" My father's gaze lifted to the mirror.

"That's Mr. Leopold in class," I explained in a bored voice. "When he gets excited."

"Bingo!" Jane cried.

"Ah. *Occurrence at Owl Creek Bridge,*" my father said.

"Right." I looked out the window. We were just turning into Jane's house. She lived at the end of a long driveway that led to a house on the shore. Her father had suddenly made a lot of money in junk bonds in Latin America, and, as Jane explained, her mother immediately set out to buy the biggest house they could find.

Lisa, another girl in the carpool, piped up, "Mr. Leopold's sooo disgusting. Did he do that in your meeting, too?"

During my meeting, he had sat still as he watched me, only absently raking his fingers through his beard—from underneath so they would appear suddenly, poking through the dark tangle of hair.

"And he had the nerve to say that I wiggle too much!" Jane said.

My father pulled around the circular drive to the front door. He stretched an arm along the seat and turned to Jane. "What's this?"

"He thinks I wiggle too much when I walk."

My father pulled his chin back in a look that could have been either disagreement or disapproval.

"Yes, he thinks I'm outrageous." She proudly recited her attributes: "I wear too much makeup. I talk too much, and my legs are way too curvy." I could see that Jane had managed to incorporate Mr. Leopold's criticism of her into her general sense of herself as being an acquired taste, the choice of sophisticates, like scotch or pâté. She got out of the car, retrieving her book bag and lacrosse stick from the back. "He told all the girls what he thought of them. Didn't Cee-Cee tell you?"

"What did he say to you?" Lisa turned to me. "I can't remember."

"Yeah, what *did* he say to you?" Jane asked, narrowing her eyes.

"You don't remember?" I said in an incredulous voice. "I'm perfect!"

My father glanced at me and raised his eyebrows, as if to say, *Well, what do you know?*

"Sure you are, Celia," Jane said, slamming the car door.

Once the car was empty and we were headed for home, I began to fiddle with the radio, scanning up and down the dial for a song I could sing along to. After a minute, my father said that if I couldn't settle on something, then to turn the damn thing off. We rode in silence until he spoke again. "So, whatever happened with that paper?" he asked. "You did hand it in, didn't you?"

"Yeah."

He lifted his gaze from the road to glance in my direction. "And . . . did he like it?" I was surprised to hear in his voice that he actually cared.

"It was the best negative review he read."

My dad leaned back, settling more comfortably into his seat. "I told you we would pull it off," he said, patting my leg. My laughter in the girls' locker room began ricocheting around my brain. A giggle escaped from my lips.

"What?"

"I." I began to laugh. "We." More laughter. "You! . . . Got a C-plus!"

"A C-plus! That wasn't C-plus work." Both hands were back on the steering wheel now. "How the hell could he possibly have given that paper a C-plus?"

"I think we were supposed to like the film. It *is* based on a famous short story."

"That's ridiculous. It was a review. Your opinion. He can't grade you down on your opinion."

"Well, he did. He's the teacher. He can do whatever he wants." The unimpeachable authority of Mr. Leopold's position hit me in a flash, and I pictured his mouth lifting in its stingy smile. And now he had authority over my father, too, I thought happily. "He does do whatever he wants," I added. "Besides, you broke one of the golden rules of reviewing, never give away a surprise ending."

"That is *not* a golden rule," my father said sternly.

We turned down our road. Our neighbor, Mrs. Parker, was outside her house again, sweeping up fallen leaves from her driveway. My dad and I had joked together about the woman sitting all day in her front window, waiting for a twig or leaf to fall so she could rush out to pick it up. "She's a force against nature, all right," I would say, which always made him laugh.

I made my joke, and he didn't laugh. We pulled into the driveway and sat for a moment in the idling car. "The guy always seemed sane enough when we chatted at school." My father turned to me. "Does this, the C-plus, seem consistent to you? Is he known to be a hard grader?"

"He's a fool, Dad. You said so yourself. He thinks I have a crooked smile."

"He what?"

"That's what he told me during our meeting."

"What else did he say?"

"Oh . . ." I looked off toward our backyard, which was strewn with leaves. "That I should stand closer to people." I arched my back slightly against the car seat, remembering the bit about not being ashamed of my breasts, but thinking of this, I felt too ashamed to mention it.

"I thought you were perfect."

"That was a joke."

My dad shut off the engine, but he didn't make any move to get out of the car.

"Are you coming?" I asked before I shut my door.

"I've never gotten a C-plus in my life."

Now I patted *his* leg. "You'll get over it," I said.

My father didn't say anything during dinner, and my mother and I kept exchanging glances and letting out quiet deep breaths.

He took a sip of wine and paused before putting his glass down, as though some thought had stalled his motion. "So,

Betsy." He turned to my mother. "Did Celia mention anything to you about that teacher, Mr. Leopold?"

"Christ, Dad. I already told you. He's insane."

My mother looked at me. "What?"

I shook my head, exasperated.

My father jerked his wineglass in my direction. "He was picking on Celia about the way she looked."

"What?" I said.

"He was picking on you?" My mother's voice was deliberate, as though her only purpose in repeating this statement was to make sure she had heard it right.

"It wasn't like that." I tried to catch my father's eye to reproach him for this exaggeration, but his glance skidded away, back to my mother. "He met with all the girls for a consultation about our appearances," I said. "It was voluntary. To prepare us for our college interviews, or something. I don't know."

"I just don't like the sound of it," my father said. "I think this guy *is* insane."

"Did the boys meet with him, too?" my mother asked.

"No," I said. "Actually, they didn't."

"Well, what did he say?"

"Just stupid stuff." Why was my father making an issue out of this now? I wondered. He had barely reacted in the car. And why was I starting to get upset talking about it?

My mother was still looking at me intently. "What kind of stupid stuff?" she asked.

"Oh, that my smile is crooked. You know, one side rises up higher than the other. And my legs would look better in patterned stockings. I should stand closer to people." Again these things sounded ridiculous to me when said out loud, and again, my throat was getting tight.

"He looked at your legs?" Once more, the disbelieving tone.

"Yeah." I snorted. "He had me lift up my skirt so he could look at my knees."

My father struck his hand against the table. "And this guy's a teacher. He's in a position of authority."

"Dad, why suddenly—"

"He had you lift up your skirt?"

"Betsy, would you please stop sitting there and stupidly repeating everything she says? I think we should do something about this. He said some stuff to Jane Raglan, too."

"And what was wrong with her?" my mother asked. She turned to my father. "If that's not too stupid a question."

"A little cheap," my father said.

"That's not what he said," I shouted. "You're twisting everything. All he said to her was that she wore too much makeup and that she talked too much. Which she does!"

My father shouted back, "Well, what this teacher did concerns me."

"Mark, stop. She's upset." My mother turned to me and touched my arm. "Honey, why *are* you getting so upset?" Then fright replaced her look of confusion. "Did he do"—she paused and continued more delicately—"something else?"

"No. No." I leaned my head forward, letting my hair fall in front of my face. "It was just embarrassing, all right? To have him point out all these things wrong with me."

"Well, what else was wrong with you? He's just one person. Can you please explain to me why this is such a big deal?"

"Ask him!" I said, pointing to my father, and got up from the table.

When my father came into my room later that night, he found me kneeling on the floor of my closet. After I'd gotten to my room, I'd slammed the door and flung myself down on my bed. I'd flipped over onto my back and stared up at the ceiling, waiting for a fresh wave of distress that never came.

Eventually, I'd gotten up and started sorting through the box of winter clothes I'd stored in the back of my closet, hoping to unearth some pleasant surprise, some sweater bought at the end of last winter and promptly forgotten, perhaps.

"I'm sorry for yelling," he said to my kneeling figure. "I shouldn't have yelled."

I shrugged my shoulders.

"You know, Celia, I really *am* concerned."

My hands were planted on my thighs, and I turned and looked up at him for a long moment. Not one lick of shame colored his solemn expression.

"Mommy and I decided to see what the Raglans think about this. It would be better to have two sets of parents complain. That would really get the ball rolling." I frowned, confused. He kept talking: "Maybe other parents would come forward, too, and then they'd have to do something."

"You want to get him fired?"

"Celia, this man keeps demonstrating some very poor judgment. With the paper, too. Yes. There's no way that was C-plus work. But, more important, this business about rating all the girls' appearances is just too much. Who is he to judge you? And what does he know about women anyway? The man looks like a troll."

It didn't quite make sense to me that Mr. Leopold's unattractiveness should disqualify his ability to judge other people's attractiveness, but before I could point this out to my father, he continued, "We are certainly not paying that exorbitant tuition so some second-rate teacher can advise you about the sort of tights you should wear."

He was still standing in the doorway, holding the knob with one hand, the other arm raised along the door frame. He seemed to be waiting for me to say something. As I looked up at him, I thought of how he reminded me of me, standing in *his* doorway, hoping for *his* approval.

I thought for a moment before I spoke. "If he's just a second-rate teacher, then why should you care how he grades?"

"That's not the point."

"What is the point then?"

"The point is." He struck the doorjamb with his fist. "The point is, your school costs me a hell of a lot of money, and as a consumer, I expect a certain standard of—an acceptable level of—"

"As a consumer?" I repeated. What was he talking about?

"What I don't expect are pompous bastards who think that being able to quote Robbe-Grillet is the height of erudition."

"Robbe-Grillet. That's the French film guy, right?" I pulled a light blue cardigan from my box of clothes and poked my finger through a moth hole.

"Celia, I'm not going to argue with you about this."

"It was just one paper. I'll make up the grade on the next one, if that's what you're worried about."

He lowered his head for a moment. When he raised it again, I could see that he had collected himself. "What I am worried about, Celia, is your education. Perhaps if you had better teachers, then you would learn how to write a decent paper, and I wouldn't have to do it for you."

I felt my stomach pitch. "That's not fair and you know it," I said, bunching my sweater into a ball and throwing it at him.

He quickly shut the door, saying as he did, "I'm calling Mr. Raglan tomorrow." The sweater bounced off the wooden panel and fell to the floor.

"You're the pompous bastard!" I yelled through the door.

"End of discussion," he yelled back as he walked off down the hallway.

But it wasn't the end of the discussion. Not by a long shot.

MR. LEOPOLD was standing at his window, looking out at a group of kids tossing a Frisbee on the front lawn. One hand rested on the windowsill, and he seemed almost wistful, as though what he was watching was something he had never known. He turned around.

"Celia. I didn't hear you come in."

"Um, do you have a minute? I wanted to talk to you about something."

He motioned for me to have a seat on the couch and then leaned up against his desk.

"It's about that paper on the movie. The review for humanities class."

"Oh, I remember it quite well," he said.

"Right." I picked at a piece of thread which had come unraveled from the hem of my skirt. "Well, the thing is, that." I kept my eyes on the thread. The thing is, I thought, that my father wants you fired, but if you just raise my grade, then maybe we can all save ourselves a lot of misery. I sighed and began again. "I didn't really think it was fair for you to grade me down just because I didn't like the film."

"Oh no?"

Glancing up, I met Mr. Leopold's eye briefly. He crossed his arms and leaned back a little farther. He looked like he was enjoying himself.

"It's not that I just didn't like Bierce's message—"

"His tired notion of death triumphing over romantic love?"

"Yeah," I said, looking back down at my lap. "But I wasn't

convinced that the guy who was going to die, the young soldier, would even have that fantasy about his wife and daughter right as he was about to be hung."

"Why not?"

"For one thing, if he were the kind of person who was thinking about them all the time, then he wouldn't have tried to blow up the bridge in the first place."

When I looked up this time, Mr. Leopold nodded, and said, "Go on."

"And I just don't believe that people are even able to think about the important stuff at a moment like that. When you're in a desperate situation, things just look more confusing. What people think about is themselves. How are they going to get out of this? How can they save themselves? Which is, actually, my point." I looked up and my gaze drifted absently around the room, as though the trail of my argument might be visible out there somewhere. I went on to critique the film's use of fantasy, explaining how even when reality is abandoned, you still have a responsibility to accurately portray human responses. How, if the story had happened in real life, the guy would have been a lot more selfish. I raised my hands toward Mr. Leopold and then let them fall in my lap. "I just didn't think the movie was convincing," I finished.

What was I talking about, I wondered. None of this was what I had planned to say. I had merely intended to make an argument that it was unfair to expect a review to have a right answer.

Mr. Leopold stroked his beard once and then stood up to go sit in his chair behind his desk. In this chair, I noticed, he looked much taller than in the one he used in class. "My question to you is, why wasn't any of this in your paper?"

I took a breath as though I were about to answer and then let out my breath in a sigh.

"Doesn't your father agree with your ideas?"

A warm flush shot up my face, and I closed my eyes for a moment. When I opened them, Mr. Leopold was staring at me. He leaned forward to intercept my gaze. "Don't play me for a fool, young lady. You think I didn't realize that you had some help on that paper?"

My hands were pressed into the couch. "He just gave me a couple of phrases . . ." I managed.

Mr. Leopold held his hand up. "I don't really want to know. I was hoping that the grade I gave you would make you think twice before going to him for help again. You don't need it. You have things to say." He gestured to the room, as though my thoughts were still hanging in the air.

"Or did your father put you up to this, too?" He leaned back in his chair and smiled. "Of course. He's upset about the grade."

"No. No. That's not it at all."

"Really?" he said, unconvinced.

"He doesn't even know I'm here," I said, glad to have some bit of truth to offer. If my father had known, he might have reconsidered charging into the headmaster's office later that morning, he might have reconsidered demanding prompt action against the "reprehensible practice of judging the girls' looks," he might have reconsidered because Mr. Leopold agreed to give me another chance. I could write the paper over, and as long as he was satisfied that it was all my own work, he would throw out the old grade. But when I called home, the phone rang and rang, and then Jane reported that she'd seen my dad in the front hall talking to the headmaster. She lowered her voice. "Actually, yelling not talking. About Mr. Leopold. Boy, your dad seemed pissed. What happened?"

I was afraid of running into my father, so I spent the rest of the morning period in the formal garden, sitting on a stone bench hidden from view by a large lumpy bush. I lit a cigarette from the pack I'd taken from Jane's locker, although smoking on school grounds could get me in almost as much trouble as plagiarism. The bench sat in the center of the garden, and as I smoked, I stared down the walkway at an old fountain made of the same pink stone as the bench. A plump nymph raised a barren urn toward the sky. I noticed for the first time that one of her feet had been broken off at the ankle.

In the front hall, along with the pictures of the old garden, was a short history of the mansion which housed the school. I'd read that it had been built in the 1850s by a railway tycoon. This tycoon had a staff of sixteen to care for his estate, six of whom were devoted to the grounds. The history detailed the many plantings which were original to the property. For almost a hundred and fifty years these shrubs had been preserved—lovingly or haphazardly, with varying degrees of skill and attention.

As I looked around at the ungainly figures, any hint of their original outlines lost long ago, I thought how of all the things that I could be sad about today, this continuance of care made me the saddest, these valiant, misguided efforts.

Ugliest Faces

BRIDGET WAS always trying to think up interesting stories about herself for Ethan. More than once, he'd said that he had to know everything about her. One time, while she was describing herself, Ethan nipped at her ears and neck and whispered that he'd like to eat her up. He would explain himself, too, but he never seemed to give it much thought, as though there was no question about the sort of man he was.

They were lying in bed one night when she told him that as a child she had almost fainted at the sight of an ugly face she had made in the mirror.

"Make that face for me now," he said, sitting up and turning on the light.

"No," she said in an affronted voice.

"Are you afraid I'll faint?"

"Please."

"Bridget, there's no face you could make that would make me love you any less. Come on, who can you be more honest with than me?"

Bridget thought of the ways she had described herself

to Ethan and how she was always trying to live up to her description.

"I can be more honest with my mother," she said finally. "She loves me unconditionally."

"How can you say that? Your mother's got all of her hopes and her dreams invested in you. When she looks at you, she's always looking for a reflection of herself. You couldn't show her the ugliest part of you because then she'd think that you'd gotten it from her."

"Well, maybe, but no matter what she saw, she would still love me. Because to not love me would mean that she didn't love herself."

"How many people do you know who really love themselves?" Ethan countered.

Often when they talked, Bridget lost the path of her own thoughts. It was important with Ethan to never show this. He was in graduate school, eight years older than Bridget, and she tried to demonstrate the great intelligence and maturity that he'd said first caught his eye when she was his student. But in many of their conversations, she felt reckless, thrusting thoughts and opinions blindly forward. She spoke fast and urgently, dizzied by what came out of her mouth; she felt as though she were balanced on the edge of a knife.

She refused to make the face for him, although he offered one of his own, rolling his eyeballs back and drawing his chin down so that his already long face looked as if caught in the grip of an invisible vise.

Her story became a joke between them, or rather something Ethan would occasionally tease Bridget about, startling her when she'd just awoken or her features were screwed up on the verge of a sneeze, saying *There it is! I saw your ugliest face!* And Bridget would laugh, a little uneasily because she sensed under Ethan's merry surface a kind of roadside curi-

osity: Was she capable of making herself really ugly? Did she
have the nerve?

ON SATURDAY NIGHT, Bridget headed out with her friend
Laurie to one of the bars frequented by undergraduates. Usually on the weekend, Ethan took Bridget on dates to jazz bars
or nice restaurants where they would share bottles of wine,
or to lectures given by his fellow graduate students from the
English department. Sometimes he would make dinner at his
apartment where he lived alone, an apartment that con-
tained shelves and shelves of books, a bed with a headboard,
not a futon or a mattress set atop a box spring, and wine-
glasses, eight of them. But this Saturday, Ethan was having
dinner with some of his friends from the Renaissance Society. "We're going to talk literature all night," he'd said,
explaining that she wasn't invited. "You'll be bored." Bridget
had considered taking offense—after all, she was an English
major—but the truth was she would be bored. Besides, when
she joined her girlfriends now for an evening out, she had a
much better time than she ever had before.

Suddenly a lot of men noticed her, and she played with
their displays of desire, challenging them to beer-drinking
contests and winning, eyeing them skeptically when they
tried to talk to her, allowing them on occasion to grope her
slyly up against the bar. Bridget had been told that she had
glorious hair; it was dark red and thick, the kind of hair that
men liked to bunch in their fists, and she would stare out at
these men from under her crown of hair and feel mysterious,
glamorous, like something they were lucky to have touch
their lives.

.   .   .

AT CLOSING TIME, Bridget leaned against the wall outside the bar's entrance while Laurie listened to a tall, lanky boy pitch his fraternity's after-hours party. Up and down the street, students poured onto the sidewalk. A couple passed by, kissing as they walked. Their mouths and tongues bobbed together and apart and together again. Bridget closed her eyes, but the darkness amplified everything—the clamor of the street, the stink of spilled beers and fruity drinks wafting through the bar's open door, the needling tone of the lanky boy. She opened her eyes and straightened up.

"Sorry, pal," she said, linking her arm through Laurie's to pull her away.

"God, he seemed so desperate," remarked Bridget as they walked off. "We were never that desperate, were we?"

"Absolutely not," Laurie said, and laughed.

In the car, Laurie fiddled with the radio, finally tuning in the Rolling Stones, "I Can't Get No Satisfaction." Bridget backed out of her parking spot and started down the side street. She and Laurie sang along with the refrain while Bridget kept time, banging one hand on top of the dashboard. In between beats, she tried to light a cigarette. The cigarette fell out of her mouth and she was bending down to pick it up when Laurie screamed. Bridget looked up just in time to see her car lift up a man. The impact carried him over the hood—his sneakers flashed across the windshield and she heard a thud as he bounced on the roof—then, in her rearview mirror, she watched him roll down off the trunk. She kept her eyes on the mirror, waiting for him to reappear. Bridget had the thought, My life will never again be the same. *Get up,* she pleaded silently. *Stand up!* How was it possible that someone had just flown over the top of her car? But already the thud of contact was a memory in her body, reverberating deep in the pit of her stomach. Bridget jumped out of the car. When she reached the man, he was struggling to his feet.

"I'm so sorry. I didn't even see you. Are you OK?" Bridget grabbed his hands to help him up. He looked down at himself and shook his head.

"Are you all right?" Bridget glanced down the street, expecting to see a police car heading their way. She was supposed to show up at Ethan's later; the thought of calling him from jail flashed through her mind, making her legs tremble.

"Maybe you should sit down," she said.

"No." She could smell alcohol on the guy's breath.

"I should take you to the hospital."

"I've been drinking," he said.

"I don't think that matters. I hit you."

"Yeah. I'm in ROTC."

"ROTC? What does that have to do with going to the hospital? You could have a concussion or something."

"No!" he yelled. "Just shut up!"

He was still holding Bridget's hands; he squeezed them and stared at her. Suddenly, he pulled Bridget to him, pressing his mouth against hers and jabbing his tongue between her lips. She waited while his tongue searched across her teeth and gums, thinking, What am I supposed to do, push him away? I just hit him with my car. Finally he broke away and she looked at him closely for the first time. He had a young and brutish face, unshaven, and slack from the alcohol, and wore his hair short in a military cut. A small fringe of dark bangs lay plastered across his forehead. They were wet with something. Blood! No, sweat or beer. He stank of beer.

"Give me your number," he said, limply pointing up one hand at her.

"R-ight," she said slowly. "You should call to let me know

that you're OK." She ran around to the passenger side of her car.

Laurie said, "What's going on? Do you know that guy?"

"Just give me a pen. In the glove compartment. And some paper. Rip off a piece of a map or something."

"Aren't you going to report this to the police?"

"And get DUI? No way."

"But we can't just leave. That would be a hit-and-run. You can be arrested for that."

Bridget looked over at him. "*He's* not going to charge me with a hit-and-run."

She gave him her number on a small scrap of paper, thinking how easily he could lose it, drop it before she even drove away. He gave her his telephone number, too, scrawling it under his name across her palm.

She lifted her hand to her face, angling it up to the streetlight. "Spite?" she read out loud.

"Spike," he corrected her. "That's what they call me at Sigma Nu."

A frat boy, she thought. A stupid frat boy. She'd been to a few parties at Sigma Nu—a bunch of rednecks and drunks.

"So you sure you're OK?" Bridget asked again before getting back into her car.

"I'll call you"—he paused and brought the scrap of paper close to his face—"Bridget."

She drove away quickly, leaving him swaying slightly on the street. That night, she lowered herself very carefully into bed next to Ethan, not even pulling the blankets over for fear of waking him. She lay awake in the dark for a long time. Her body kept tensing, remembering the dull jar of her car hitting Spike and the quick, thorough search of his tongue through her mouth.

.   .   .

ETHAN HAD WAITED until the semester was over to ask Bridget out, a point which he mentioned repeatedly as though this forbearance was a source of pride. When Bridget told her version of the story, she would say in a coy voice that not one thought of romance ever crossed her mind when she was his student. Which was the truth—she'd been shocked to learn of his interest in her. She had never felt intelligent or mature in his classroom; she was too tongue-tied. From the very first meeting, she had noticed how desirable Ethan was, eventually seeing that he knew this about himself. He wasn't particularly handsome, but somewhere along the line, he'd realized that women found him attractive, and he'd acquired the confidence of a handsome man. He took it for granted that everyone sought his attention, and as a result, people were always trying to entertain him.

Ethan's attention was irresistible to Bridget. She wasn't sure why she'd been chosen, but whatever Ethan thought he saw in her, she certainly wasn't going to give him any reason to amend his opinion.

She opened her eyes to find Ethan propped up on his elbow, staring at her. Behind him, the morning sun filled the white curtains with an opaque light. She pressed a hand to her head, trying to hold still the dull pain throbbing there. Ethan brushed his fingertips across her eyebrow, smoothing the hairs into place.

"You didn't wake me last night," he said.

"No." Bridget turned her face away from his hand. Thank God, she thought. If he had waked, she might have blurted out everything. She could guess what Ethan would make of it—she wasn't mature; she was reckless and dangerous. And how could she explain kissing Spike? That she felt she owed him something, that he'd taken her by surprise, that his advance was so outrageous as to be oddly thrilling? She turned onto her side, away from the bright windows and

Ethan, hoping that if she didn't answer, he would think she'd fallen back asleep.

His hand lightly touched the back of her head. When he spoke again, his tone was uncharacteristically uncertain. He told Bridget that he liked it when she came home a little drunk and woke him in the middle of the night.

"It's nice to see you getting so much pleasure from my body," he said, combing his fingers through her tangled hair.

"Hmm," Bridget answered. What would Ethan say if he knew that on those nights his body could be any body, or even a pillow or a bunched sheet?

"So, how was your night?" Ethan's tone was still cautious, as though it were he instead of Bridget who hadn't been invited along the evening before.

She thought of the crowded bar, the boys sitting across the table from her, trying to make her laugh; the way she would pause before answering a question, knowing that they would wait. She thought of walking down the street with Laurie, swaying against her, laughing, relieved at being able to leave behind the boys and their parties, their raw and greedy hunger. And then the thud of contact and Spike's kiss—tasting the hunger on his tongue.

She uncurled her fist and looked down at her palm. Although she'd washed her hands before coming to bed, the inked scrawl was still faintly visible. Spite, she thought. Perfect. He probably doesn't even remember what happened. He's probably still asleep in the frat's driveway, the car radio left on. Ethan's fingers paused in her hair. She heard him take a breath and then hold it as though he had decided against whatever it was he was going to say. She squirmed backward until she was pressed up against Ethan's body.

"I find that scene kind of depressing now," she said.

He let out his breath and his fingers began their lazy

movement again. "It's too bad you didn't come last night," he said, his confident tone restored. "I didn't realize . . . well, some of the guys brought their girlfriends. You would have enjoyed it. Bright interesting people."

"Maybe next time," she said, brushing her cheek against his forearm.

He rubbed his hand up and down her arm. "I can't imagine what your life was like before we met."

Bridget closed her eyes briefly, pleased at this moment not to be able to imagine it either.

Ethan rolled onto his back. "God," he said, his voice now melancholy. "Who did you talk to?"

BRIDGET RETURNED home to find a note from her roommate, Allison: *Messages for you on machine.* As Bridget waited for the tape to rewind, her heartbeat quickened. Both messages were from Laurie, wanting to know if Bridget had heard from Spike, or if she'd had a call from the police.

"Jesus Christ," Bridget said when she got Laurie on the phone. "What were you thinking, leaving all that on the machine? What if Ethan was here?"

"You didn't tell him?"

"No. Of course I didn't."

"Better he find out now than when you call him from down at the station."

"Would you please just relax? That guy was so drunk he's not going to remember who or what hit him."

"He's got your phone number, Bridget. And he knows that you were with someone. An accessory. I'm involved in this, too, you know."

To her surprise, Bridget realized that Laurie was afraid of being left out. "The guy's in ROTC," she said. "They're not supposed to drink. He doesn't want to get into trouble either."

"But what if he's not OK. What if he had an aneurysm or something, and he died."

"An aneurysm? Jesus, Laurie, are you *trying* to get me in a state of panic? Because you're doing a pretty good job."

"I just think you should call him to make sure he's OK."

Bridget didn't say anything. She knew Laurie was right.

"And then you better call your parents."

After Bridget hung up, any optimism she felt quickly evaporated. She sat down in a chair. Her knees were shaking. I *could* call him, she thought. I could just call him, see if he answers, and hang up. She looked at her palm. She couldn't make out his phone number anymore. Thank God she'd thought to write it down before going into Ethan's apartment.

"Yeah?" was all the voice said when answering the phone. Bridget waited a few seconds before replacing the receiver.

She went upstairs to her bedroom to dig out her freshmen directory. She searched through the pages of photos, but she didn't know Spike's real name or what class he was in. Any one of the young men's faces—their expressions set blankly for the camera—could have belonged to him.

A FEW DAYS passed, and Bridget hadn't heard from Spike. She still hadn't told Ethan what happened, finding it exhilarating to keep this secret from him. She was more playful than usual, teasing him a lot and bossing him around, frolicking at the edge of this private catastrophe she had begun to imagine she had escaped.

.   .   .

ONE AFTERNOON a few days after the accident, Bridget bumped into Laurie in the library, chatting with a student. "This is Kevin," Laurie said, and then added pointedly, "he's a Sigma Nu."

Bridget just smiled and nodded.

Laurie gestured to Bridget and said, "We met a guy in Sigma Nu the other night. What was his name?"

"I don't remember," Bridget said coolly.

"It's a pretty big frat," Kevin said. "Does he live in the house?"

"He's in that military thing," Laurie said. "What is it? RO—"

Kevin held his hands out to his side. "Kind of a stocky guy. Spike?"

"That's it," said Laurie. She went on to say how drunk Spike had been and wondered if he was OK.

"I think he has the flu," Kevin said. "He's been in bed all week."

Then Laurie asked what Spike was like, and Bridget gave her a look meant to sear her mouth shut.

"Oh, he's a sicko," Kevin said, sounding slightly proud. "You should see what he makes the pledges do. He's scares the shit out of them."

"Jesus." Laurie glanced at Bridget. "Has he ever done anything to a woman?"

"No," he said, dismissing her suggestion. "I've never seen him with a girl. I don't think he'd know what to do if he found one."

When Kevin left, Laurie swung around to face Bridget, her expression taut with excitement.

"This isn't *Melrose Place*, Laurie," Bridget said, shaking her head. "This is my life you're messing with." As she walked away, she added, "When are you going to fucking grow up?"

.　　.　　.

ON SATURDAY MORNING, Ethan and Bridget drove to Boston to the wedding of one of his classmates. During the ride down, Ethan entertained Bridget by describing the various dancing styles of his fellow academics. The groom, Hank, was a modernist: antitraditional, nihilistic, antiaesthetic. "When Hank dances, he punches at the air like someone shadowboxing." Ethan let go of the steering wheel to demonstrate. "He makes no effort to be on the beat. In fact, he's *trying* not to be on the beat." He described Hank catching himself with each step, as though he were reinventing the language of movement. Bridget looked out the window and frowned. Snow spotted the roadside—compact brown piles like bits of rubbish that had been swept up and would soon be carted away.

"I can't imagine anyone who puts so much thought into it being a good dancer," she said finally. "The trick is to try to forget what you're doing."

Ethan looked at her and smiled. He waited, as though he expected her to say something else. After a moment, he said, "Of course, he doesn't *actually* think about all these things. I was, you know, riffing a little."

"Right," she said skeptically. Later she realized that Hank's dancing was not so unusual or inventive. He was simply someone who lacked any sense of rhythm.

Bridget didn't get a chance to see what Ethan's dancing was like. Each time the other couples rose from their chairs and headed for the floor, she glanced at Ethan, waiting for him to stand and reach for her hand. But instead he would frown and make some comment about how awful the band was. Finally Ethan's friend Nick stood up and motioned to Bridget. "Come on," he said. "You should get at least one dance tonight."

With a hand pressed to the small of her back, Nick steered her through the cluster of tables. He bent his head and said in a low voice, "Your boyfriend doesn't like to do anything that might make him look foolish."

Over dessert, Bridget became the center of attention. Everyone at the table took turns peppering her with questions about fraternity parties and sorority hazing, the drugs that undergraduates took nowadays, the amount of sex they had. Were her friends racists? Political? Intent on making a lot of money? Bridget relayed rumored stories involving vomiting and group showers; she bemoaned the materialism of her peers, their conventional tastes and lack of interest in politics. All the while, Ethan nodded encouragingly.

In the elevator ride up to their hotel room, Bridget remarked to Ethan that his friends seemed to like her.

He snorted and said, "They acted like you were a visiting emissary." But Bridget knew from the attention Ethan paid her when they made love that he thought the evening had been a success, too.

When he rolled over to his side of the bed, Bridget fell back against the pillows. The lights were off, and she lay in the dark, lost in the disquieting moment of reclaiming herself. Her arms and legs felt heavy and useless, her hair limp against her cheek. The air was cold on her damp skin, and she sat up and fumbled around the foot of the bed for the covers. She wrapped herself in a blanket and stared out at the room. She couldn't remember what it looked like. With the shades drawn, she couldn't even make out the opposite wall. Ethan's breathing deepened as he drifted off to sleep. She lay back down and closed her eyes, but she couldn't get over the feeling that she didn't know where she was. Her urge to click on the light was almost irresistible.

She told herself that she was being silly, that she knew exactly where she was. Just an hour or so before, she'd been in the hotel ballroom four flights below, dancing and drinking and talking with Ethan's friends. Yes, she said to herself, casting about for a comforting thought, think of entertaining Ethan's friends. But remembering how she'd maligned her peers, panic replaced the feeling of superiority she'd had, as though she'd forsaken the only allegiance she could claim.

She felt dizzy and put her hand to the night table. If she could just see where she was. She sat up and clicked on the light. The sight of her purse and jacket on the chair calmed her.

"Are you all right?" Ethan asked, propping himself up on his elbow.

"I feel a little light-headed. Too much wine, I guess."

"You look pale."

Bridget got out of bed, avoiding his gaze. "I'm going to get some water."

She shut the bathroom door and looked at her reflection. She *was* pale. The faded red of her lipstick provided the only color in her face. She thought of the story she had told Ethan, about the time she almost fainted; she'd been looking in the bathroom mirror then, too. The vividness of her recollection—like a snapshot she had just stumbled upon—made her wonder if it was the story rather than the black anonymous room that had propelled her from the hotel bed. She remembered now that she had been home sick with a fever that day (she must have been ten or eleven years old at the time), and had been asleep for most of the afternoon, dreaming that her parents and teachers kept metamorphosing into monsters. When she'd gone to the bathroom for a drink of water, her image in the mirror had been blurry and exaggerated, as if she were wearing 3-D glasses. She'd made different faces, watching herself grow more and more unfamiliar, thinking that eventually she would be able to look upon herself as a stranger and see herself truly. Stopping on one face, she'd held it and strained to twist her features even more. Her skin had grown hot, her head wobbly. Slowly, she'd sunk to the floor. Only after a few minutes of breathing deeply with her head between her knees had she been able to stand again.

She hadn't told Ethan all of this, only the part about making the face and almost fainting. That's when he'd said, "Make that face for me now."

Bridget thought how when people share strange stories about themselves, the expectation is that the story becomes diminished, but actually the exact opposite is true. Putting a story on record places it on the compass of your being, a point always to approach or flee.

THE NEXT DAY, more messages were waiting on the answering machine. A voice she immediately recognized as Spike's said that he heard she'd been asking about him—she reached for the volume control to lower it—and how they needed to talk. Damn Laurie, she thought. Goddamnit!

He answered on the first ring. He said that he had gone to the hospital the day after the accident, and that he had multiple contusions.

"Well, I'll pay your hospital bill, of course. Just tell me how much."

"My leg is pretty messed up, Bridget. I might lose my ROTC scholarship."

"Jesus. But you said you were OK. Do you remember that?"

"Well, I'm not. I think you should come over so we can talk."

"I don't see why we can't discuss it on the phone."

"Look, Bridget, this is pretty serious. I think you should come over."

"I'm busy right now. I have class."

"Then it will have to wait till tomorrow. I'm not going anywhere."

When they finished talking, she replaced the phone in its cradle gently, although there was no one home to overhear her.

THAT AFTERNOON, Bridget waited for Ethan in the graduate lounge in the English department, trying to read *Hamlet*. Next week, Nick was delivering a paper, "Get Thee to a Nunnery: A Study of Chastity in *Hamlet*," and Ethan had suggested that she would enjoy it more if she had read the play. But she couldn't focus on the text. She kept wondering how she was going to spend a whole evening with Ethan without telling him about Spike and his phone call.

Ethan glanced quickly around the lounge to make sure they were alone before bending down to kiss her hello. He announced that they'd been invited to dinner at the house of one of his friends. Apparently she'd been a hit at the wedding.

"I wouldn't miss it for the world," she said a little too enthusiastically, shutting her book with a snap.

BRIDGET WAS hardly inside the door before someone took her coat. She handed it over, and suddenly Nick was in front of her, leaning to kiss her on both cheeks. "Like in France," she said as she pulled apart from him, laughing. The hostess, Katherine, who had spoken with Bridget for a while at the wedding, pressed a glass of wine into her hand, saying how glad she was that Bridget could make it. Ethan headed toward the living room, reaching his arm behind him for

Bridget's hand. The eight or so dinner guests were scattered around the room; everyone seemed to be talking at once.

"Lord, look what the cat dragged in!" A tall woman with cropped black hair rushed toward them. Ethan let go of Bridget, and the woman hugged him for a long moment. Bridget smiled vaguely around the room, looking for people she recognized.

"Sylvie, this is Bridget." Ethan put his arm around Bridget's waist and pulled her forward. Sylvie shook her hand, meeting her eyes with a gaze startling in its intensity. Bridget glanced down to her wineglass and then raised it to her lips.

"So, Ethan," Sylvie turned back to him, "I was just at a party in Manhattan where your name was being bandied about."

"Oh yes?" he said, interested.

"I thought you would like that," Sylvie said. She and Ethan started talking about a couple whom Bridget had never heard of. She listened for a while, nodding along as the two chatted, then eventually found an open spot on the couch. She sipped her wine and put her glass down on the coffee table, thinking that tonight would be a good night to drink slowly.

AT DINNER, Bridget found herself seated next to Nick. She thought about telling him that she was reading *Hamlet* in preparation for his paper, but worried that he would make the same incredulous face Ethan did when he learned that she hadn't read a particular book.

Wine bottles passed around the table, everyone topping off their glasses, while the men tried to outdo one another toasting the food and hospitality.

At the far end of the table, Ethan was deep in conversation with Sylvie. He lifted his head and said loudly, "We'll put it to the table. What's the greatest sin you've ever committed? How about you, Nick, what's yours?"

"Being your friend, I would say," Nick answered.

Everyone laughed and Sylvie said, "Hear! Hear!" raising her glass.

"Seriously. This is a serious question." Bridget looked up from the piece of bread she was buttering and Ethan caught her eye. "You're up next," he said, nodding at her.

"Well, I suppose I've committed some sins in the name of seduction," Nick said, raising his wineglass to his grinning mouth. No one spoke while he sipped, swallowed, and smacked his lips. Finally, he dabbed at his mouth with his napkin so gingerly—as though he were dusting some fine porcelain figurine—that Bridget had to fight an urge to rip the napkin out of his hand and tell him to get on with it. "But I won't bore you with the details," he said at last. Over the chorus of boos, he called out that most everyone present had probably heard enough about his sinning already. Bridget remembered Ethan telling her that Nick had seduced a number of his students and broken a few of the poor girls' hearts along the way.

Nick turned to Bridget. "You're too young to have committed any great sin."

She'd just taken a bite of the bread and in the time it took for her to swallow, the table quieted and everyone turned to her. "Don't be too sure," she said, straightening in her seat. She thought about answering that she was Ethan's girlfriend, but it fell flat when she said it in her head. Everyone was waiting. "Once I hit a person with my car." The words were out of her mouth before she even thought about them. The gay mood in the room vanished as swiftly and completely as if Bridget had stood up and shut off all the lights.

"Were you trying to run someone down? An old girlfriend

of Ethan's maybe?" Nick asked finally, a nervous chuckle in his voice.

"Actually, it was a guy. I didn't know him."

"You didn't kill him, did you?" Ethan asked. He turned to Sylvie. "Only *I* would fall for a murderer."

"Of course not," Bridget said, rushing to her own defense. "I just drove away." Everyone at the table burst out laughing.

"Ah," Sylvie said. "So your sin would be cowardice instead of murder." Bridget saw that the amused smile Ethan had held during the meal was gone, leaving his face long and serious. "Everyone at this table is a coward," Sylvie continued. "That's no great sin."

"I mean I didn't drive away immediately. I made sure he was OK first. He seemed fine. He was really drunk, so it was hard to tell, but he could walk and everything." Bridget kept glancing over to Ethan as she talked, but only Sylvie would meet her eyes. She felt as though she had to explain herself to them both. "In fact, I found out later that he *was* fine," she lied. "Just a minor concussion, that's all."

"Well," Sylvie said when Bridget was finished, "*my* greatest sin would have to fall under the heading of adultery."

"That's old news," Ethan said, amused once more.

Sylvie went on to tell a story about sleeping with her best friend's boyfriend in college, as though she were the first person in the world to do that. Bridget wasn't really listening. She was thinking of all the other answers she could have— she should have—given when it was her turn.

"And you, Ethan? What would be your greatest sin?" Nick asked. Bridget prayed that Ethan wouldn't say anything that involved her and required a retort. She finished off her glass of wine, which Nick obligingly refilled.

"Well, you've all known me long enough by now to know that I'm absolutely perfect!"

"Conceit," Nick said. "I should have known."

After dinner, Bridget excused herself to go smoke a ciga-rette. "I don't mind smoking in the house," Katherine said, starting to get up from the table. "Let me get you an ashtray."

"Don't be silly." Bridget was already out of her chair. She put a hand on Katherine's shoulder. "I could use some fresh air," adding quickly, "I mean my lungs could."

She stood on the porch with her back to the party. Occa-sionally, she heard the conversation's volume swell and be-come swallowed by laughter. She could pick out Ethan's laugh, hearty and insistent. She heard the door open behind her.

Sylvie stepped onto the porch. She smiled at Bridget sheepishly as though she had some bad news that she was looking forward to delivering. But she didn't say anything. She just gazed out at the night, rocking back and forth on her heels. Bridget turned away to survey the party through the living room window. "I love dinner parties, don't you? Ethan and I should throw one. It's such a civilized way to socialize."

"Definitely." Sylvie touched Bridget's arm and gestured to the cigarette pack cradled against her ribs. "May I have one?

"So, have you two been together long?" Sylvie asked once she had lit her cigarette and exhaled her first drag in a loud, satisfied sigh.

"Oh, awhile. Three months, at least. He's wonderful. He's endlessly interesting."

"You think so, huh?" Sylvie nodded her head and smiled. "I bet he likes that." She raised her cigarette to her lips.

"Well, he's also endlessly interest*ed*. He can't seem to get enough of me. He drives me crazy sometimes, but we're really, really happy."

"Then I am very glad for you. Both of you."

Bridget wondered when and for how long Sylvie had dated Ethan. Maybe they just slept together once or twice. He wasn't above that, Bridget knew. As he'd said, sex was one way of discovering if you were compatible with someone, and if you're not, there's no sense in prolonging things. She's probably terrible in bed, Bridget thought—too studied and careful. God forbid she ever made a mistake or did something embarrassing. She was just like Ethan.

Sylvie didn't say anything more. She just stood and smoked, raising her face, exhaling the smoke from her mouth, curling it up into her nostrils and then letting it escape slowly into the air. Bridget was growing tired of watching this act when an image of her own face reflected in a mirror sprang before her, her lips twisted to one side, her nose scrunched and eyes squinted. She shook her head, as though to clear it.

"Sorry to leave you alone out here," Bridget said finally, "but I've got to get inside before I freeze to death."

"Of course." Sylvie nodded toward the door.

ON THE WAY HOME, Ethan sped along the winding back roads, straddling the middle line on curves, barely pausing at stop signs. Bridget watched the hunched, dark outlines of the trees lining the street zoom by and felt sick. She leaned back against the headrest, but had the feeling of being pressed backward, as though she couldn't keep up with the speed of the car.

She lifted her head and asked, "Will you please slow down?" The words felt slushy in her mouth.

Ethan tapped the brake a few times, then turned to her. "You're the naughty girl, aren't you." Even in the dim glow of the light thrown off the dashboard, Bridget could see the mischief dancing across his face.

"What?" She took a deep breath.

"You never told me about hitting someone with your car."

"Oh that. It was a long time ago."

"It couldn't have been that long ago. You've only been driving for three years, right?"

"Well, it feels like a long time to me." Bridget turned toward the window and, closing her eyes, pressed her forehead against the glass.

"It didn't seem that way from how you talked about it. Your voice was shaking."

She mouthed the words *I give up, you win.* Bridget pictured telling Ethan everything—about hitting Spike and his shoving his tongue into her mouth, about his call and his insistence that she go see him. She didn't even want to think about what he wanted from her. And if she told Ethan, he would make sure that she never found out. He would be happy to comfort her, she knew, happy to tell her that he would take care of everything.

She leaned back from the window and opened her eyes. He'd sped up again. "Christ, I told you to slow down!" she yelled. He jammed on the brakes, pitching her forward so she had to throw her hands up to catch herself on the dashboard. They were quiet for a moment and then Ethan looked over and said, "You know, you really should be wearing your seat belt."

THE NEXT MORNING when Bridget walked into the fraternity house, everyone was at class. Spike's room was on the third floor. The door was slightly open, but she knocked anyway. Spike was lying under the covers with the sheets pulled up to his chest. He wasn't wearing a shirt and she couldn't tell if he was wearing anything else. She noticed on the top of the covers a magazine picturing a soldier on the front and she almost smiled.

She stood with her hands in her pockets at the foot of his bed. "How are you feeling?"

"I told my sergeant I've got the flu. I'm not sure how long he's going to believe it."

"What about your leg?"

"Do you want to see it?" He started pushing the covers down.

"No. No. That's OK. I believe you," she said quickly. She looked for a place to sit down. There was a couch across the room facing away from the bed and then a chair closer by, covered with clothes.

"Sit here." He patted the edge of the bed. She sat gingerly, as if it were filled with quicksand. She didn't take off her coat, although the room was warm. Sheets were tacked over the windows, blocking out most of the light and any fresh air. The room smelled ripe.

"Look Spike. I feel really bad about what happened. You should have called me right away when you found out about your leg."

"I've been thinking about you all week," Spike said.

"Well, if you knew me, you'd know that I'm a responsible person. I want to be reasonable with you."

"You're pretty," he said.

"Thank you." She willed herself to not look down as she did when Ethan complimented her. She waited, fidgeting with her car keys still clutched in her hand.

"I had to fill out a police report at the hospital before they would treat me. If I gave them your name, you'd get charged with a hit-and-run."

"But I offered to take you to the hospital. You remember that, don't you? You wouldn't go."

"I remember everything," he said.

"So you know that I didn't run away."

"You're supposed to report any accident to the police; otherwise it's a hit-and-run. Didn't you know that, Bridget?"

She looked away from him because she couldn't stand his

gloating smile. "So what are you going to do?" she finally asked.

"I just want to talk a little. I'm really not a bad guy. Why don't you take off your coat? It's so hot in here."

She sighed impatiently, shrugging her coat off, and said, "I have class soon. I can't stay long."

Spike asked her what year she was, what courses she was taking, where she went out at night. He chatted with her as though they were at a party and they had found themselves standing next to each other. "So, do you have a boyfriend?" he asked.

She was going to answer that it was none of his business, but then she thought it would be good to let him know that she was taken. "Actually, yes. He's a graduate student. In English. His name is Ethan." Ethan's name on her lips sounded silly, soft and lisping.

"Is he nice to you?"

"Of course." Bridget looked at her watch, trying to remember when the morning class period was over and the other fraternity brothers would be coming back. "Look Spike. I'm really sorry. I wish it had never happened. But I don't know you and I don't really want to know you. I don't even know if you're telling the truth."

"I'm going to show you what you did to me." He started to lower the sheet, and Bridget pressed her hands down on the bed, ready to push herself up and run out of the room. He was wearing boxer shorts, faded blue from many washings. From his upper thigh down to his knee, his skin was purple and black and spotted with bursts of red. She reached her hand out to it, involuntarily, as though toward a beautiful vase on a table. Spike caught her hand and raised it up so it rested on top of his boxer shorts.

She could feel his penis, semi-erect, jump, announcing its

presence. She removed her hand slowly and then buried it in the safety of the folds of her coat. "Spike," she said quietly, looking down.

Then he reached up to touch her breast through her sweater, stroking around her nipple, searching until he found the tiny display of excitement. Bridget watched what he was doing and felt as though it were happening to someone else. *She* would have outwitted him, talked him away from this outcome, stood up and left, risking whatever consequences came. She looked up and Spike was staring at her. He looked as surprised as she did about what he was doing and the fact that she hadn't stopped him. She pictured herself getting up and walking out, and she knew that if she did, she would never hear from Spike again.

But she didn't walk out. She stayed, closing the door and locking it when he asked her to. She sat back down on the bed, took off her sweater for him, and unclasped her bra. "I don't want to get you in trouble. I'd never want to get you in trouble," Spike whispered, almost like an afterthought, as though to give them both a reason to explain what was happening. Bridget let him pull off her jeans and underwear. She spread her legs and he positioned his head between them. Looking up from between her thighs and meeting her gaze, he asked her to tell him what to do.

"This is humiliating," she said, staring back at him. "You realize that, don't you? You're humiliating me."

"Tell me what to do," he repeated.

And she did. "Yes. That's good," she said and then, "A little lower," and finally, "Use your finger now. Yes, now."

"Well," Spike said after she came. "I guess we're even."

Bridget laughed despite the situation and said, "I don't know how you figure that." But she didn't wait to hear his answer because she realized that he knew this had cost her something. "I don't want you to call me again, Spike. If you do, I'll tell everyone what happened. I'll tell them you black-mailed me."

Bridget stood up, pulling her jeans and underwear back on. Reaching behind her for her sweater, she felt suddenly light-headed, a familiar wooziness sneaking up from behind her eyes. She sat back down on the bed and leaned her head forward, willing herself to hang on. Spike reached out to clasp her shoulder, asking her if she was all right. She straightened and brushed his hand away, pulled her sweater on, and left without looking back.

Rather than walk down through the house and risk seeing anyone she knew, Bridget left by the fire escape. She pushed open the heavy metal door, and the bright noon sun blinded her for a moment. When her eyes adjusted to the light, she saw that the whole campus was visible from this height, from the empty bleachers surrounding the football field to the flat-roofed concrete dormitory where she lived her fresh-man year. She started down the three flights, the iron stairs trembling beneath her, the metal ringing with each step.

A Day in the Country

My father liked to pretend that he and my best friend, Kelly, had a secret joke—he would whisper in her ear, and then they would both burst out laughing. Whenever I asked her about it, she would tell me that he wasn't saying anything, just mumbling gibberish. My mother thought it was nice that Kelly and my father got along so well since Kelly didn't get much attention from her own father. Kelly's parents were divorced, and her father lived in a different state; the most constant men in her life, besides my dad, were her mother's boyfriends.

Kelly and I watched the Saturday morning cartoons while we waited for her mother to emerge from her bedroom down the hall to drive me home. She had her newest boyfriend in there with her. The night before, Kelly and I had been lying in Kelly's bed, not yet asleep, when we heard him come in. He was nice, Kelly said, but he had a big mustache that tickled when he kissed her good-bye. We wiggled around in her bed, making retching sounds and screeching under our breaths, "Eewh, gross, yuck," at the idea of mustaches and kissing. "Ssh," Kelly said, putting a finger over my lips. I froze; my eyes widened, and I waited for whatever would come next. Her head was raised off the pillow and cocked to one side. She turned to me and grinned. "Sometimes, I can hear them," she whispered.

I perched on the edge of the off-white sectional couch, unable to keep my mind on the cartoons. Kelly was stretched out on the floor in front of me. I jumped up and headed down the hall toward the bathroom for the third time that morning. The white shag carpet muffled my footsteps as I tiptoed past Kelly's mother's bedroom door. During my last trip, I had heard the boyfriend laughing. Now I put my ear to the door and there was only silence, a frightening absence of noise, and I knew that they were doing it at that very moment on the other side of the door. These words, *doing it,* aroused a shameful flush of satisfaction.

When I walked back into the living room, Kelly didn't even look up from the TV set. I didn't understand how she could pretend that nothing was happening. I felt like a dangerous slippery animal was running loose in the apartment, and as desperate as I was to catch it, so I could at least see what it looked like, I was terrified of its rubbing up against me.

Suddenly, Kelly's mother was standing in the living room doorway. The handles of two coffee mugs dangled from her finger. She wore white cutoff shorts and a T-shirt I recognized as an old gym shirt of Kelly's. The shirt rode up over her slack belly.

"Morning, girls," she said and then glanced at me. "Why don't you get your stuff together and I'll drive you home."

Kelly nodded to my overnight bag by the front door next to my sneakers and said, "She's been ready to go for hours, Mom."

.   .   .

KELLY CLIMBED into the backseat of her mother's car with me. We were headed down High Gate Road out of town when she whispered in my ear that two nights ago James had called her. I looked out the window so Kelly couldn't see my face. James went to the same day school as Kelly and myself, though he was in the eighth grade, a year ahead of us. He also happened to live near me, and sometimes I would talk to him while he threw a ball for his dog in the field next to my house. A few times, I had invited him over for a Coke or to watch TV, but he always had some reason he was expected back home.

"He wants to come over to your house tonight." Kelly grabbed my arm to get my attention. "And he's gonna bring his friend he met at Deerfield summer school. So I'm gonna ask my mom if I can sleep over, OK?"

"Well, I have to ask my mother first," I said. "We're having company for dinner. My dad's friend is coming out from the city for the day."

Kelly giggled and hugged herself. "He was so cute on the phone. He kept putting his dog on and trying to get him to bark."

"Sheba," I said. "I've met her. It's a girl."

"Whatever."

When we turned down my street, I spotted my father down the road walking toward our house. I had the car door open before we had even reached a complete stop. "Thank you, Mrs. Marcella, for having me over," I said, grabbing my bag off the seat. "Call you later, Kelly. Bye!" I slammed the car door and dropped my bag in the driveway to run down the street to greet my father.

"Whoa! Careful now," he said, as I jumped up at him, wrapping my arms around his neck and letting my body go weightless. He took me in his arms, groaning, and staggered a few steps. "How's my three-hundred-pound baby?" he asked.

"Terrible. Mrs. Marcella had her new boyfriend over so we had to watch TV for hours until she came out of her bedroom to drive me home."

My father put me down and turned to watch the Marcellas' car pull away. "She has a new boyfriend, huh."

We headed past the brick walk leading to our front door. Only certain visitors—my father's friends from the city or musicians or divas from the opera company where he was a conductor—used that entrance. The front door was painted dark red and on it hung a large black knocker in the shape of a lion's face. When someone rapped with the ring hanging underneath the lion's mouth, a deep, majestic knocking sounded throughout the house, which I loved for its affirmation that both our home and the visitor were very important. The Marcellas had one of those musical doorbells, three long notes, which seemed stupid to me because they lived in an apartment of only four rooms, and all the other apartments in their building were just like theirs, so it wasn't special at all.

"What's this boyfriend like?" my father asked.

"He's got a big mustache." I made a face.

"Is he younger than her?"

"I don't know. Why? Do only younger men have mustaches?" I linked my arm through my father's so he could escort me through the kitchen door.

"Sometimes when a man grows a mustache, he's trying to look older. Of course, he also could have something wrong with his lips."

My mother looked up from the kitchen table where she sat. "Who's got something wrong with his lips?"

"Kelly's mother's new boyfriend," I said, plopping down in a chair next to her.

"That's too bad," my mother said and returned to her *House Beautiful*. "She's an attractive woman," she added, flipping quickly past photographs of airy rooms and teeming gardens, "although I can't understand why she insists on dressing like she's twenty years younger than she really is." To the magazine's pages, my mother offered an embarrassed face, as though Mrs. Marcella's taste in clothes somehow implicated her.

"All divorced women do that," my father explained. "They forget how to be sexy while they're married and then suddenly they're single and the only way they can think of to attract a man is to get themselves up like a teenager." He selected a piece of apple from my mother's plate and chewed it thoughtfully.

"I would *never* dress like Mrs. Marcella," I said.

"No you won't," my mother said. "Not while I'm still paying for your clothes."

"So, you'll never guess what Mrs. Becker told me on my walk today," my father said.

"Goodness. What now?" my mother asked, looking up from her magazine.

"Margie's lost another four pounds. But her bosom, her mother happily reports," my father paused, lifting his hand to his hat and shaping his fingers around its crown, "hasn't shrunk one bit." He removed his hat and dropped it onto the table.

Margie Becker went to my school also; she was four grades ahead of me and had the biggest boobs in the whole school. Her family lived down the street.

My father laughed and continued, "So her mother and I are standing there leaning up against the split-rail fence talking about Margie like she was some new horse they'd just gotten. Next I'll be hearing about her bowel movements!"

The Beckers had three horses, one of which was an older, very tame chestnut that Margie used for giving riding lessons to some of the girls in the neighborhood. At the beginning of summer vacation, I had begged my father to let Margie give me lessons, too, but he said that there was no way he was going to pay five dollars an hour so I could sit on top of a smelly animal and walk in circles.

"What I'm wondering," my mother reached for my father's hand, "is what you ever said to make Mrs. Becker tell you about Margie's dieting all the time. You didn't say anything when Margie started getting so chubby last winter, did you? No jokes about needing to get her a bigger horse, I hope." She picked up a slice of apple. "Well?" she demanded, jabbing the fruit up at him.

"Of course not," my father said. "Mrs. Becker just realizes that I'm a concerned neighbor. And I am. I would hate to see Margie go to fat."

"You're so mean," I said, giggling conspiratorially.

My mother lifted her head to my father. Her long blond hair fell back from her face, accenting the sharp-boned handsomeness of her profile.

My father bent down and directed my mother's hand and the apple slice to his lips. He opened his mouth wide around her fingers and bared his teeth. Then he closed his mouth down on her and moved his head back so his lips slid along her fingers, stealing the fruit away with a soft sucking sound.

"See how mean I am, Lily," he said after he swallowed. "I was going to bite your mother's fingers off. But then I thought, Who's going to do the cooking and the cleaning? and I changed my mind."

"Da-ad," I said, stretching the word out into two syllables to let him know that I didn't fall for this kind of joke anymore. My father ran his hand through his wavy brown hair, fluffing it a little where it had been flattened.

"All right," he said, retrieving his hat from the table, "I want to get some work in before Alfred comes." He hung up the hat on the row of hooks in the hallway and headed down the basement stairs to his music studio, closing the door behind him.

My mother groaned. "It seems like Alfred was just here, doesn't it? It can't be more than a few weeks since his last visit."

"I remember school wasn't out yet, so it's got to be at least a month."

"Well, the day your father stops feeling indebted to him will not come soon enough for me." She stood up, clasped her hands, and stretched them toward the ceiling, arching her back and rising on her toes. Before she married my father, she had been a ballet dancer, and she still moved with the grace and self-consciousness of someone who was always aware of having an audience. She strolled over to the pantry door, opened it, and with one hand on her hip, peered inside.

"What am I going to make for dinner. Let's see. He'll eat spaghetti."

"But no fettuccine, lasagna, noodles, or any other form of pasta," I answered.

"Right. Red meat," she went on.

"Only if it's very lean."

"Butter sauces are OK."

"And cream sauces are definitely not," I said, putting on my television announcer voice.

"No paprika." She grinned over her shoulder at me. "His impoverished childhood in Hungary. And no garlic or mush-rooms in anything, absolutely ever." She closed the door and sat back down. "Do you think if I stopped indulging him, he wouldn't visit us anymore?"

"We're his only friends," I said, quoting my father. "The only ones who will put up with him."

"Yeah. Yeah," my mother said wearily.

"Besides, he did put Daddy on the map, and in the Met, for that matter." Now, I was quoting her.

My mother cradled her chin in her palm and narrowed her eyes at me. "Since when do you remember everything we say?"

"Make lamb chops with mint jelly. I love the way you do those."

"A good suggestion. God, I hope his new girlfriend isn't a vegetarian. They get younger and wackier with every visit."

"Oh, I almost forgot," I said. "Kelly's sleeping over tonight."

My mother raised her eyebrows as if she were considering saying no.

"Don't worry. We'll get her mother to drop her off."

"All right. So, do you want to go to the supermarket with me?" The pitch of my mother's voice rose, as though this were a fun proposition.

"Umm. Not really."

She sighed and turned back to *House Beautiful.* "I don't know why I always get stuck with all the work around here." And I left her there, flipping through the magazine's pages again, before she could ask me to do anything else.

I CALLED KELLY from the family room. As we chatted, I could hear the television still going in the background and the sound brought me back to the smallness of her apartment, the whiteness of its carpet, walls, and couch—how easily everything there could be soiled. I considered inviting her to spend the whole day over, but I liked hanging around with my parents and their friends who came to spend a day in the country. On these days, familiar activities—lounging by the pool, meals, adult conversation—were transformed into luxurious novelties, and I was afraid that Kelly wouldn't know enough to appreciate them, that she would just want to hang out in my room all day and talk about James. I told her to have her mom drop her off after dinner.

"OK. I'll call James to tell him that it's all set. And Lily," she added before she hung up, "his friend is supposed to be really cute."

I stared out the window at the field next to our house. I thought maybe I would spot James out there with Sheba. I was pretty sure that Kelly planned on kissing him tonight. Lately, she had been making me practice with her a lot, and recently she'd said that she thought she was ready.

We always practiced at my house in one of the changing rooms in the pool house, lying on an old couch. With a handkerchief held between our lips, we would press our mouths together and wiggle our hips against one another. Sometimes Kelly would wrap her arms around my back and clutch me tightly against her, and through the thin cloth, I would feel her lips part, and her breath, warm and heavy, against my mouth.

These encounters always left me feeling slightly stunned, conscious of an aching inside my body that was started on a slow, gentle arc and then suddenly shunted off just as it was climbing the upward slope. Kelly, on the other hand, would break apart from me abruptly, neatly refold the handkerchief to be put back in our hiding place for the next time, and give me her criticisms in a businesslike voice: I still needed to move my head more or I was panting through my nose again.

Before Kelly made me start practicing, when I thought about boys I wouldn't think about smushing my mouth against theirs. Sometimes I would stroke the skin right above my hips which I thought incredibly soft, and I might imagine taking a certain boy's hand and having him touch this secret bit of soft skin. This seemed to me the kind of thing, quiet and gentle, you did with someone you liked.

A Day in the Country

I got up and opened one of the sliding glass doors. My mother's garden was in full bloom. A honeysuckle vine climbed up a trellis set against the house, and its languid sweetness filled the air. The roses were bursting red, hanging pendulously on their vines. Bright pink gladiolus stood tall, waving slightly in the light breeze, and large ferns spread, wide and protective, behind them. The week before, a woman from a local paper had come over to photograph the garden. The woman put my mother in some of the pictures, posing her in front of her flower beds in a big straw hat. Since my father was a well-known conductor, people sometimes took an interest in my mother, too.

All the careful arrangement of the garden made my eye search for something out of place: dead flowers, a clash of colors, a broken stalk, but I couldn't find anything. The heat of the noon sun had burned through the morning's haze, and now the sky was unwaveringly clear. I stepped back inside, shut the door, and headed upstairs to change into my bathing suit. I wasn't going to let the thought of some boy keep me from having fun today.

MY MOTHER and the girlfriend lay in lounge chairs by the pool. The girlfriend's name was Beth; so far that's all I knew about her. She was looking up and frowning, or maybe squinting in the sun. My mother was putting on suntan lotion, gliding her hands languorously up her forearms, as if she were putting on opera gloves. The lotion's coconut scent drifted in the air.

Alfred bent down to retrieve the football. Earlier, my father had persuaded him to remove his linen sports coat. Alfred wore a white cotton shirt; its back and sleeves were very wrinkled, as if only the front had been ironed. Sweat made the shirt stick to him. He had also removed his shoes and socks and rolled his pant legs up a turn or two, revealing feet and ankles that were white and thin.

"Toss it here," my father called, "and I'll throw one for Lily."

"All right," he said once he had the ball. "This one's for the game." He cocked his arm back and glanced to his right. I started to run. He pulled his arm back farther, and I accelerated. The football spun fast through the air and then suddenly it was dropping into my arms. I folded them closed, the ball trapped safely against my chest.

"That's my girl!" my father called. I heard some clapping and glanced over to my mother, but she wasn't even looking. She was talking to the young girlfriend.

I slowed down and trotted past my father. "The ball, Maestro," I said, spinning it to him underhand. "I'm gonna jump in. Want to join me?" Right as I said this, I remembered that my father didn't like to swim. He said he had poor buoyancy.

"Umm. Not right now. Maybe later," he answered, pretending not to notice my mistake.

"Right-o, Pop."

I jogged over to the pool and then onto the diving board and . . . stopped. Something marred the blue bottom. A blurry spot of white, speckled with tan and brown. A bird, I thought. A bird, drowned in the pool. I was about to call out for my father when the water rippled and the shape moved slightly, extending out into a crumpled napkin. I dove in and swam to the bottom to fish the napkin up.

"Look, Mom. One of your linen napkins was at the bottom of the pool."

"Oh, the wind must have gotten it. Bring it here." My mother stood up, yanking the bottom of her bathing suit back into place.

I swam over to the edge and held the napkin up. Once my

mother had hold of it, I pulled. She jerked forward, but I hadn't pulled hard enough for her to lose her balance. "Gotcha!" I said. "Come swim with me."

"Maybe later, Lily."

"Come on, Mom. Daddy threw the ball with me." I pulled on the napkin again, harder, but this time she was prepared. She yanked back and my stomach was scraped against the pool's concrete edge. I let go and she stumbled backward a step. "Fine. Don't swim with me," I said, pushing off from the side with my legs and then kicking hard to splash her.

I floated on my back out to the center of the pool, watching my mother turn to my father and gesture toward me as if to say *Did you see that?* He smiled and said something, shaking his head, but with my ears beneath the surface of the water, the only thing I could hear was my own breath. I listened to it more closely and noticed how ragged and loud it sounded, reminding me of a sound track from a scene in a movie when someone was being chased. I arched backward and dove down toward the bottom of the pool, where I thrashed back and forth, wrestling with a slippery monster, fighting with all my strength, until I couldn't hold my breath for one more second. I came bursting up out of the water, gasping for air, and swam limply over to the shallow end to sprawl across the pool's stairs. When I'd finally caught my breath, I lifted my head to see that everyone was heading over to the table to start on lunch.

LATER IN the afternoon, we moved inside to the living room. My mother appeared with a tray, carrying a bottle of white wine, glasses, and some orange juice for me. On the coffee table, she had already laid out a platter of cut-up vegetables and dip, and some crackers and cheese.

Beth made room for my mother to put down the drinks.

"You're such a wonderful hostess, Ellen," she said. "I could never do all the things that you do." Beth was a painter.

"Well, I'm sure you could if you put your mind to it. But thank you. It *is* something I enjoy."

Beth accepted a glass of wine and continued, "I find most women my age are hopeless when it comes to homemaking. It's a shame, actually. I mean, just look at the lovely home you've created, the splendid lunch, your gorgeous garden." She peered out the living room window. "They're almost little works of art themselves. I don't know the first thing about any of that."

My mother looked at Beth curiously, as though trying to decide whether Beth was being stupid or nasty. She poured herself a glass of wine and said, "Once you get married, you'll learn soon enough."

"Well, I'm not sure *that* will happen in the near future." She glanced at Alfred, but he was talking to my father. Sometimes, after Alfred's visits, my parents would discuss how he was never going to settle down, my father sounding a little wistful and my mother's voice edged with disapproval. Now my mother just shrugged as if to say *Who knows?* and sat down on the couch next to Beth. I moved to the floor near the coffee table so I could reach the food more easily. I especially liked the artichoke dip, and I kept loading it on my celery stick and then licking it off. The sun slanted in the western window and lit up the couch in front of me as though it were on a stage.

"I've started calling her Kitty because she's up all night like a cat," Alfred said, putting his arm around Beth.

"I have trouble sleeping," she explained.

"Besides, she's not really a Beth, is she? *Is she?*" Alfred entreated my father. Beth smiled and leaned back, resting her head against Alfred's arm. She had changed into a stretchy black dress; it was quite short, and whenever she shifted positions, the dress crept up her legs. I could see her thigh dimpling against the sofa cushion. Clumps of sequins dotted the front of the dress. Something that looked like a small mirror was sewn over her right breast. When Beth first sat down, Alfred had leaned forward and pretended to look in this mirror, fussing with his thinning hair. Kelly's mother had a similar dress, without the sequins, though, which Kelly and I sometimes took turns trying on. Both of us were too little to fill it out, so we would pinch the extra fabric behind our backs while we sashayed in front of the mirror.

"We can do better than 'Beth,' I think," my father said.

Everyone turned to consider her and she took a series of deep gulps from her drink. Her dark burgundy lipstick was slowly transferred to the rim of her glass. She had a heart-shaped face, and her eyes were set high and wide apart. When she pursed her lips to take a sip, she looked a little like a doll I used to have whose face was fixed in a permanent pout.

"How about 'Claire'?" my father suggested. "Soft, but forbidden, like a rich dessert." I wondered if my father was thinking of éclairs, which we both liked. He continued: " 'Adele,' daring and sexy. 'Marguerite,' French like her almond-shaped eyes, and exotic. 'Lena' or 'Anita.' " He said this last name in a Spanish accent, tossing his hands up in imitation of the commercial that was currently on TV for a Broadway musical.

"Evita!" I called out the name of the musical and threw my hands up, too.

" 'Lola,' " he finished in a low growl.

"Ooh! I like that one!" Beth squealed, clapping her hands. During his litany, she had been wiggling around, shifting positions with each new suggestion, and her dress had risen up even more, reaching the very top of her thighs. Alfred started telling a story about a woman he once knew named Lola.

"How about a name like Brandy or Sherry," my mother said. "Something sweet and harmless, like a little after-dinner drink. But do you like after-dinner drinks, Beth?"

Beth pulled her skirt down, freeing it from underneath her behind with a little bounce. She turned to look at my mother over her shoulder and said, "Why sure. A little drink after dinner can be nice."

"Oh no," my mother said. "I'm afraid we don't have any. We never drink anything stronger than wine." She lowered her voice and sat forward, leaning close to Beth's shoulder. "Luke is always worrying about contaminating his mind. I suppose what he's worried about is that his work will become contaminated. He even refuses to socialize with some perfectly nice people who he says are unbearably pedestrian and contagiously dull." My mother laughed. "I've never seen him drunk in fourteen years of marriage. Do you worry about that? Contaminating your art, I mean?"

"No, not really," Beth said. "I don't worry. I figure any experience is just grist for the mill."

"Oh!" my mother exclaimed. "Luke, did you hear that?" And then again, "Luke!" louder this time. My father looked up. "Beth just said 'grist for the mill'! Isn't that a wonderful phrase? I can't remember the last time I heard it."

"Grist for the mill. Grist for the mill," I said in a singsong voice. It *was* fun to say. "But what does it mean?" I asked.

"Something that's advantageous, Lily." My father turned back to Alfred.

"I hear people say it all the time," Beth said. "Actually, quite a lot," she added. "At the school where I teach art, they say it."

"Yes, that would make sense," my mother said. "Teachers

love those phrases that make everything sound so positive. They're very reassuring."

"I don't see what's wrong with that," Beth said, speaking through a smile.

"Why, absolutely nothing," my mother said emphatically.

Beth reached forward to cut some more slices of cheese. Our faces were quite close, but she didn't show any sign of noticing that I was right in front of her. She arranged the slices on pieces of cracker and then, after she had restored the smile to her face, she got up to offer the plate to my father. "Are you starving over here? Or are you too busy talking with Alfred to notice?"

My mother watched Beth, tapping her fingers against her glass as though she were deep in thought. My father waved the plate away. "Ellen"—he turned to my mother—"we should think about taking our walk soon. Do you need to do anything in the kitchen before we go?"

"I do, as a matter of fact." She stood up. "Lily, do you want to come help me?"

"Do I have to?"

"Of course not," my mother said, sounding disappointed, and walked out of the room. I thought about getting up to go help her after all, but she had looked a little angry when she walked out, as though my father had sent her out of the room. Besides, I wanted to find out if I could really see myself in Beth's little mirror. I got up and plopped down on the couch next to her. The wine in her glass sloshed a bit and a little splashed over the rim onto her dress.

"Shit," she said under her breath.

"Oh, I'm sorry," I said, reaching for some napkins. "At least it won't show. Since it's black, I mean."

"Yes. That's true," she said brightly, like someone who is used to mustering up forgiveness. Before she turned away, I leaned my head down to look in her mirror, but all I could see was a flesh-colored blur. Alfred and my father were talking about a violinist whose name often came up when they were together. Beth nodded along as though she knew this man, too.

"My friend Kelly," I said to Beth, "her mother says that if you wear all black it makes you look skinnier."

She glanced at me. "Well, I don't have to worry about my weight."

"But isn't it true that you look skinnier wearing black?"

"I just happen to like the color," Beth said and turned back to Alfred. "So in that review of yours recently, you thought that his playing had fallen off lately, gotten a little too pressured. Isn't that right?"

"Yes?" Alfred raised his eyebrows.

"Well, that's so interesting," Beth said, quickly sipping her wine.

"Yes," Alfred said again and turned back to my father.

"But black isn't even a color," I said, tapping Beth. "As a matter of fact, it's the absence of color. Don't you like colors? I mean since you're a painter. Or do you only paint in black and white?"

"No, I work in colors," Beth said.

"But you don't like to wear them," I said triumphantly.

She leaned forward and put her glass down on the table. She studied the tabletop as though she were looking for something. Abruptly, she sat up, planting her hands on her knees, and faced me. "I don't always wear black. Oh, never mind." She leaned back on the couch and then, after a moment, sat up again. "I've got to use the powder room. If you'll excuse me?"

"Of course," I said, flattered that she had asked my permission.

. . .

MY MOTHER WAS on the telephone when I went into the kitchen to get her for our walk. She sat in a chair facing the window, her body hunched forward as if she were protecting the phone receiver. "Yes. Yes. I know all that, but I have a thousand more important things I should be doing." She looked up and waved me out of the room. I marched in place, pumping my arms back and forth, and then beckoned her. "Hold on a second," she said into the receiver. "Just go without me. Tell them I've still got to make the dessert."

I stopped in the doorway of the living room. Alfred's hand rested on Beth's thigh and he was leaning forward as if about to kiss her. Luckily, I looked away just in time. My father came down the stairs. "Everybody ready?" he boomed.

MARGIE SAT TALL on top of the chestnut in the middle of the field that stretched beside the Beckers' house. Jumps of varying height dotted the grass. She wore a black T-shirt and dark brown breeches the same color as her riding boots. "How svelte you look perched up there, Margie," my father said. Alfred squinted across the field at her, reminding me that he was nearsighted.

We all leaned up against the wooden split-rail fence.

"I used to ride when I was young. God, I remember getting the worst calluses on my ass," Beth was saying in a loud voice to no one in particular.

Margie was talking with my father. He had asked her if she could take all of those jumps. "Of course," she answered and then asked if he wanted to see her do it.

"Why yes. We would like that very much," my father said with a sweep of his hand to indicate the rest of us.

Without a moment's hesitation, Margie chucked the horse in the ribs twice and started off. They trotted around the perimeter of the field. She didn't post as I had watched girls do at a riding school I had once visited with a friend; she clung to the saddle, rising and falling with the horse's movements as she steered him toward the line of jumps. My father, behind me, rested his hand on my shoulder. As she took each jump, his grip tightened, as though he were the horse himself, pushing down on me to launch himself upward. Now maybe he would understand why I wanted to learn how to ride.

After the last jump, he started to clap. She trotted over to where we were standing and stopped the horse right on the other side of the fence.

"Well!" My father turned to Alfred and Beth. "How about that!" he said proudly, as if he were responsible for the display. I reached up to pat the sweaty animal's neck and cooed at him: "What a good boy. Nice horsie."

"Yes, very nice," Alfred said, looking over both Margie and the horse.

"I never got to jumping," Beth said with a sigh.

"What do you think, Lily," my father asked, leaning forward to peer at me. "Would you like to learn how to do that?"

My hand froze in midpat. "But *you* said—" I turned to my father in disbelief.

"Actually," Margie said, "I do have an opening right now. Cindy Dunn, you know," she pointed vaguely behind her, "I was giving her lessons, but she just left to go to some jewelry-designing camp out in New Mexico run by real Apache Indians."

Margie smiled at me more kindly than she ever had before. "Would you like some lessons, Lily?"

"But Dad—" He had straightened up and was looking over my head at Margie on the horse.

"She really ought to know how to ride," my father said, and then finally looked in my direction. "Right, Lily? Why live out in the country if you're not going to ride horses!"

Margie swung down to the ground. "You can give him a try right now, if you want."

"Yes. Let's see my girl up on a horse."

Margie began shortening the length of the stirrups. My father, his hands on his hips, looked on. He grinned at Beth and Alfred, then he grinned at me, clearly delighted with this turn of events. A shudder ran down the horse's flank, and his tail flicked up to brush at a fly. I was struck suddenly by the animal's enormous size.

"I don't want to," I said, taking a step backward.

"No reason to be scared," my father said, placing a hand on my back to prod me forward again. "He's not going to bite you."

"I said I don't want to."

"Well before you said that you *did* want to learn how to ride. I guess I should stop paying attention to things you say."

The beginnings of tears sprang to my eyes, and I lowered my head.

"A lot of girls are scared of him at first," Margie said. She gave the horse a few loud smacks on his side. "But he's a lamb. You should see him—"

My father broke in abruptly: "Well, enough of this dilly-dallying." He seized my hand—"On with the walk"—and called thanks to Margie as he led us away.

We turned down a side street. James's street, actually. James. Tonight. The friend. I just wanted to go home, but my father held my hand tightly in his grip as he pulled me along.

He told Alfred and Beth about his encounters with Mrs. Becker. He stretched the story out, describing how she would always run out from the barn when she spotted him, sometimes still carrying a pitchfork in her hands. How she would jab the pitchfork into the earth and then rest one arm on it, wiping the sweat from her brow with the other.

"She's probably never met anyone famous before," Alfred said, scornfully.

"It's strange she never rides herself," my father said. "Neither does the husband. Anyway, Margie's been losing all this weight, and every time I see her, her mother gives me the latest update, as if I'm actually concerned."

Alfred laughed and said, "When I was a child in Hungary, my family always arranged to buy a turkey once a year from a farmer whose son attended my school. All the time, the son, whose job it was to care for the birds, would talk to me about how fat our turkey was getting. This boy wanted to be my friend, you see, because I was the smartest boy in the school, and he told me how he made sure our turkey was fed very well and wasn't exercised too much so it wouldn't be tough. When we finally got the bird, I found I couldn't eat it. I knew it too well. Which was a shame because turkey was considered such a special treat."

So? I wanted to say. *What does that have to do with Margie?* But I didn't say anything. Although my father still held my hand, he seemed to have forgotten that I was there.

"Quite right," my father said, "but instead of fattening her up, her mother is slimming her down."

"How much weight has the girl lost?" Beth asked.

"Oh, twenty, twenty-five pounds over the last three or four months."

"Really?" Beth said, leaning across Alfred toward my father.

"In outfits like that tight T-shirt she had on, you can almost make out her rib cage."

"Well, she has an eating disorder, of course," Beth said.

"What?" my father said.

"Yes," Beth insisted. "No one loses twenty-five pounds in four months without starving themselves or throwing up. I see it all the time at my school. Her parents must be blind."

"No doubt," my father said.

"Perhaps you should have a talk with them."

"Oh," my father said, sounding impatient, "I don't think so."

"Gross." I made a retching sound. "Who would ever make themselves throw up on purpose."

"It's a very serious problem for young women," Beth said. "Don't you get any ideas, Lily. It's very bad for you. Very bad."

"Lily would never do a thing like that. She knows that she's perfect just the way she is." My father reached down and wrapped his arms around me. I leaned into him, relieved to have been forgiven, and buried my face in the softness of his cotton shirt and its familiar, comforting scent. His hands started to dig closer, searching for my ticklish sides, pressing until it hurt. "There's Lily's ribs. No fat here."

"Stop!" I cried, jerking away.

After another minute of walking, Alfred announced that he was getting hungry. When I saw that we were approaching James's house, I chimed in, "Me, too."

"I hope Ellen's made something that I can eat," he added.

"For Christ's sake, Alfred," Beth blurted out. "Do you have to always sound like such an old man." She turned to walk back toward the house.

WHEN WE GOT home my mother told me that Kelly had called and that she would be over in a couple of hours. "I invited her to dinner, but she's going out to eat with her mother and the new boyfriend. Kelly seems to think that this one is serious. Apparently her mother really wants her to get to know him." My mother laughed. "I do think it's strange how Kelly's mom talks over her love life with her daughter." My mother seemed in a better mood than before. I had often noticed that when she got off the phone from talking with one of her friends, she seemed more carefree, as though some balance had been restored.

Since I felt bad about having left her alone, I offered to set the table. When I was finished, I went back into the living room. My father was standing by the stereo.

"Mom says dinner will be ready in a few minutes."

"Which means about twenty minutes," my father said.

"Oh, I should go offer to help," Beth said, hopping up.

"I already set the table," I told her. "Too late."

"Well, then I'll insist on doing the dishes." She sat back down.

In the kitchen, my mother had complained about Beth's not offering any help. "I know better than to expect anything from your father or Alfred, but you'd think *she* would at least try to make herself useful."

My father pulled out a record that he wanted to play for Alfred, one of the Afro-Cuban records that he liked to listen to when he relaxed. He said these people knew more about rhythm than anyone. When Alfred visited, my father often played him Afro-Cuban music, but he could never be persuaded of its value.

"You say it's primitive, I say it's plebian," Alfred said this time, raising his voice to be heard over the sound of the drumming.

Beth stood in the middle of the room, as if we were playing a game of charades and it was her turn to pantomime a phrase. My father began clapping out a rhythm which didn't mimic the beat, but followed it in some way. Beth tapped her foot in time to the music, experimenting first with a steady tempo that closely followed the beat. Then her foot tapping grew more elaborate, stuttering taps interspersed with heavy stomps. She translated this complicated tapping into a walk across the room to my father, who was still clapping, until she was standing right in front of him.

He raised his hands to chest level. Beth added her hips and shoulders and head to the rhythm that she was keeping. All the parts of her body were moving in different directions but were somehow coordinated. Sometimes my father would put on opera music and practice his conducting, and my mother and I would twirl around the carpet, acting out the opera, but this wasn't dancing like that. Alfred stretched his arms out along the back of the sofa so his hands almost reached from one end to the other. I didn't want him to touch me, so I leaned forward a little. He was making quiet little snorts of amusement. Beth started to spin around, still keeping up her dance, and my father walked around her in a circle, clapping high and low.

I jumped up and started hopping around on the carpet, weaving in between them. I sang a song my father had taught me, "If you see a guy wearing all kinds of ties, you can bet that he's doing it for some doll, some doll, some doll, some doll." And I kept repeating "some doll" until my father told me they'd heard enough.

Beth flung herself into Alfred's lap, but he didn't move to embrace her. My mother poked her head into the room, scanned it quickly as though she had left a bunch of children here and was surveying the damage, and then announced dinner. On the way into the dining room, I overheard my father telling Alfred that you could learn a lot about rhythm from Beth, too.

KELLY'S MOTHER dropped her off just as we were starting the lemon meringue pie. My father pulled up a chair for Kelly, and my mother served her a slice. Kelly reached for my hand under the table and squeezed it. "Eight-thirty," she mouthed. I pulled my hand away to take another bite.

"Why, Kelly," my mother said, "is that lipstick you're wearing?"

"Yeah. My mother let me put some on in the car."

"How grown-up my little girlfriend looks," my father told her. I thought she looked silly, like her mouth was stained from drinking grape juice. The word "cheap" popped into my head as though it had been whispered to me by my mother.

"So tell us about the new boyfriend," my father said. "I hear he sports a mustache."

"Yeah. It looks sort of funny, I think. My mom's totally in love. He's come over every night this week."

"Sounds like love to me," my father said. But I knew he wasn't right about this, and that if he had been there this morning listening outside Kelly's mother's bedroom door, he would have known exactly what it was.

"Come on, Kelly," I said, getting up from the table. "Let's go watch TV."

We went into the family room. Kelly reached into the pocket of her jeans and pulled out a tube of lipstick.

"My mom let me keep it," she said. "Do you want to put some on?"

"No thanks."

She got up and went to the bathroom. When she came back her lips were dark and shiny, and her hair was brushed and arranged so it fell in smooth waves in front of her shoulders. She perched on the edge of the sofa, not leaning back, so as not to muss up her hair. I was thinking about telling her that she could go off with James without me, that I wouldn't be mad; that they could go to the pool house if they wanted, and I would just wait here with his friend, but then I heard the loud knock at the front door.

I led the boys into the dining room to introduce them. James's friend, Ted, shook everyone's hand, looking them right in the eye. He was cute enough, but nothing really special. He asked Beth if she was enjoying her visit.

"I'm just visiting myself," he said. "I go to Deerfield Academy in Massachusetts."

"That's a very good school," Beth said.

"Yes, it is," Ted answered.

I took the boys into the living room. Ted told me that his parents collected antiques, too. "We have a hutch like this." He and I were standing in front of a tall painted hutch with various pieces of earthenware arranged on it. Kelly and James were on the couch. She was telling him about going out to dinner with her mother's boyfriend.

"My parents' hutch is worth five thousand dollars," Ted said.

"Well, I'm sure that this one is worth that much, too."

Ted wanted to know what my father did. When I told him that he was a conductor, he asked if his parents would have heard of him.

"He's been at the Met, you know, in New York City," I said. "He's very well known among people who know about music."

Ted said that he'd thought about becoming a musician, but he wasn't sure if there was much money in it. James and Kelly were giggling. She punched him playfully in the arm. James looked up at us.

"Are you two having an intellectual conversation?" James asked. "Ted likes to have intellectual conversations."

"Hey, Lily. James wants to show us something out in the woods behind the Beckers' house," Kelly said.

"What do you want to show us?" I asked.

"You're just going to have to come and find out," James said.

"I already know about the tree house back there. It's been there for years."

Ted piped up, "Hey, I'd like to see a tree house."

"What? They don't have them in Massachusetts?" I said.

Kelly gave me a look, her eyes narrowing. "Just go tell your parents we're going out, Lily."

I walked back into the dining room and told my parents we were going out.

"Where are you going?" my father asked.

"Just out for a walk."

"With those two boys?" Beth asked, smiling.

"Yeah, they're coming."

"Well, they seem like decent boys," my mother said. "Beth was just telling us how competitive Deerfield Academy is. That Ted must be a very smart young man."

"I guess," I said, lingering over the table.

"Have fun," my father said, and then turned to my mother. "Ellen, don't you think Alfred would like some coffee before heading back to the city?"

KELLY HAD me smuggle two beers out of the house, and we all took turns sipping from them. She kept talking about how dizzy she felt. We stood in a little circle at the base of the big maple in which the tree house was built. I made a half-hearted suggestion about climbing up to see it, but no one responded. Ted threw his empty can on the ground, crushing it with his heel. Everyone seemed to know what we were there to do. I wondered if Kelly and James had actually discussed it beforehand. A fallen log had been placed near the base of the tree as a sort of bench, and I kept jumping on top of it and then back to the ground. Finally Ted spoke up, "Lily sure is a funny name for a tomboy like you." I thought about telling him to call me Lola then, but I had already decided to pretend that I wasn't even there, so I didn't say anything, just hopped faster.

Finally Kelly said in a very grown-up voice, "Oh. What the hell," and walked up and gave James a kiss on the cheek. I stopped jumping and watched her. It didn't last very long, but she kissed him with a big smacking sound as if he were a baby, not at all like the kind of kisses we had practiced. She then stood just behind James's shoulder, so close that I thought that he could feel the warmth of her breath on his neck. All he had to do was turn around, and the next time it could be their mouths that met. Then they would have a real kiss, and I knew that that kiss would be a sort that I had never seen.

Ted looked at me and waited, tilting his head up to where I stood, still on top of the log. "Well?" Kelly said, her insistent breath warming the back of James's neck. I looked down at my feet, and then to the ground below. Kelly sighed, walked up behind me, and placed her hand on the middle of my back, applying the gentlest pressure. I curled my toes in my sneakers, setting my stance on the log more firmly, and raised my hands to my sides for balance. Ted took a step forward and steadied himself, as though he expected to have to catch me before he'd get to actually kiss me. No one spoke as they waited to see what I was going to do. The only sound came from the Beckers' barn behind us, a low neighing, resolved and melancholy. I wanted to jump down and dodge past Ted to run back to my house. There, I would take up my spot on the living room floor again, watching and listening to my parents and their friends as they sipped their coffee, the last ritual of a day in the country. Then again, Kelly's voice came, whispering in my ear this time, "It's your turn, Lily," and her voice—with its slight edge of authority and note of impatience, as though what she were pushing me toward I had been heading to all along anyway—reminded me of my father's, but I knew that *he* would never surrender his girl so

easily. Kelly prodded me harder, and I began to lose my balance. As I fell into the arms of this boy in front of me, I
thought of my mother and of Beth and Margie, too, and wondered what they would do in my place, and it seemed that the
only choice I had was to hope that this boy would be able to
catch me.

Snowed In

LILY KNELT on the leather couch to look out the window. Seven more inches had accumulated over the night, erasing any evidence of the snowball fight from the evening before, and still the snow kept falling. A thick white blanket was draped over the garden benches, the boxwood hedge, the lawn jockey at the end of the front walk—only his lantern held high over his head could be seen above the drift. A row of evergreens lined either side of the long driveway, and mounds of snow weighted down their boughs, prying them back from the trees' black trunks. From between these trees, a bright red Jeep Wagoneer appeared, sped up the driveway, and fishtailed to a stop. Lily recognized it as Bobby Callahan's car. She dropped out of sight.

None of the other girls sprawled around Cristal Harlow's den had even glanced up from the television screen. Lily settled against the soft leather cushions without mentioning the new arrivals. She pictured how the back of her head was framed by the window, and a small chill ran through her, making her shiver slightly.

Around the other side of the house, not visible from here, was the stone wall where Bobby had run up behind Lily the night before. She'd been scooping snow together, compacting it into balls between her mittened palms, when Bobby had rammed his body against hers, pushing his hips into her, pressing her chest and face forward into the pile she'd made. She'd known it was him behind her even before he'd whispered *You're mine* in her ear and dumped a fistful of snow on her head. Then he'd pushed off her and run away as quickly as he'd come, with Lily's consciousness, it seemed, fleeing with him—she didn't notice the cold wetness against her hot cheeks; she didn't notice the snow working its way inside the collar of her ski jacket until a trickle of icy water ran down her spine, returning her to her body with a start. She'd bolted up and arched backward, brushing frantically at the snow lodged against her neck. And then outrage jumpstarted her brain. She gathered up as many snowballs as she could and began running toward the intermittent screams and *Gotcha*s circling through the darkness, running with the unswerving fury of someone who held her target in her sights.

Of course, all evidence of that encounter was gone as well.

From outside came the sound of car doors slamming and boys' raucous laughter. "Is that Bobby?" Cristal hopped onto her knees to peer out another window. "He's with Eric and Kyle. And they brought more beer. That's so nice. They brought one, two"—she mouthed *three*, then *four*—"wow, five cases."

Lily watched Cristal out of the corner of one eye. Kneeling on the couch as she was, her hands planted atop the sofa's back, her big butt waggling slightly as she spoke, Cristal reminded Lily of a large, plump dog. She would have liked to lay a hand gently on the girl's arm, to tell her to sit down, to . . . contain herself more, but if she did, she knew that she would hurt Cristal's feelings. Lily picked up a copy of *Gourmet* magazine from the coffee table and began flipping through its pages.

Daphne, on the other hand, sat up in the leather recliner she'd commandeered. "Get down, Cristal," she said. "Do you want them to think we've been staring out the window, waiting for them all morning?"

"But she—" Cristal began, glancing at Lily, who was studying a recipe for potato leek soup. Cristal sighed and flopped back down onto the couch. "Well, I'm glad Bobby came back. I knew he would." She turned her head to look out the window again and then stood up. "I better go make some room in the fridge if we're going to fit all that beer in."

Daphne frowned as Cristal headed out of the room, but she kept quiet. In the cavernous leather recliner, Daphne looked smaller to Lily than her five feet and ninety-seven pounds. But not frail. Even with her pinched little face and wispy short hair, she could never look frail. To be on the safe side, Lily always regarded her as a few degrees short of an explosion.

Courtney and Nicole were also lounging around the den. None of the girls at Cristal's house were particular friends of hers. Lily wasn't close with any of them either, although Courtney sometimes palled around with her at parties. Courtney was pretty, with long blond hair and a full red mouth that was usually fixed into a flirty smile for some guy's benefit. The boys paid attention to Lily, too, which was the reason, she imagined, that Courtney often stuck close by her.

And Lily hardly knew Nicole. She had just arrived at their school at the start of the second term. Some business venture of her father's had brought them here from England. So far, she'd moved among her classmates as distant and queenly as a Persian cat who had accidentally wandered into a barnyard.

Snowed In

. . .

IT WAS spring break, and the thing that brought the group together at Cristal's house was that they were the ones who had been left behind. The rest of the eleventh-grade class at Woodbridge Country Day was off visiting grandparents in Palm Springs or Boca Raton, or helicopter skiing in Utah or sailing the Caribbean in chartered yachts with their parents. Back home, the snow had been falling on and off for two days now, and Cristal's parents were away—her father on business in Hong Kong and her mother, Cristal said, at a health spa, although it was common knowledge that she was regularly checked into detox.

And so anyone who was around made their way over to the Harlows' house—some of them borrowing a family car and then arranging to stay the night with the explanation that they were snowed in; Lily, who lived only a few miles away, had come on cross-country skis. Her parents were happy to be rid of her complaints—*There's nothing here to eat; There's nothing to watch on TV; There's nothing to do.* She could stay as long as she wanted.

COURTNEY stood up, saying something about having to use the bathroom, although Lily knew that she was going to brush her hair. At the other end of the couch, Nicole continued to file her nails. Lily wondered if she should go help Cristal, but she didn't want Bobby to think that she was anxious to see him. From the kitchen, rising above the sound of jars clanking and cardboard boxes being torn open, she could hear his voice describing in great detail his daring maneuvers through the snow on the drive over. Lily twisted her hair up into a loose bun atop her head and then teased out a few tendrils of hair to drape along her face. So what if Bobby was the cutest boy in their class or if he was the first thing their basketball and soccer teams ever had that resembled a real athlete. She wasn't interested.

WHEN LILY heard someone coming down the hallway, she bent her head to her *Gourmet.* Filling one whole page was a photograph of a steaming slice of peach pie.

"Oh, please," said Nicole in an exasperated voice, and Lily glanced up to see Bobby holding out a can of Miller Lite. He had planted himself in between Nicole and the television.

"What's the problem? I got Lite especially for you girls."

"I don't care if it's Lite or not. I don't drink beer."

"Oh, right, Miss Fancy Pants. Only champagne for you," said Bobby, jutting his nose in the air. Lily lowered her head to hide her smile. "Well," he continued, "I can't help you there.

"Beer here, beer here," he said in the nasally voice of the beer sellers at Yankee Stadium. He shuffled over until he was facing Lily. She leaned to one side to peer around him and he moved over to block her view. She leaned the other way and there he was in front of her again. He took a step forward and very slightly inclined his hips toward her.

"I know you want it, Lily," he said. She looked down at his feet. The room, it seemed, had abruptly gone silent, but inside she was pitching wildly, and any possible retort was whisked from her reach by these stormy currents.

Bobby spoke again: "Here you go." A can of Miller Lite appeared in front of his zipper.

She snatched the beer from his hand and, without thinking about it, found that she could speak after all. "Move, Bobby!" Adding more softly, "Please." She lifted the can and took a long, deep sip.

"Starting early, aren't we, Lily?" Daphne said.

Courtney walked in, trailed by Eric and Kyle, all carrying cans of beer.

"So where's mine?" Daphne demanded. When she received no answer, she yelled to Cristal in the kitchen. Finally she got up and went in there herself.

Bobby plopped down on the leather recliner. "Ah," he said, leaning the chair back, "it's good to be the king."

Kyle sat down in between Lily and Nicole. He bumped his shoulder against Lily's. "Bobby didn't tell me you were going to be here," he said.

Lily raised her eyebrows and took another sip of her beer. Kyle was still looking at her. "Well, here I am," she said finally and turned back to the TV.

THE WEATHERMAN predicted another ten to sixteen inches of snowfall in the next twenty-four hours, and a reporter, his red face peeking out from a large dark hood, appeared on the side of a highway. Over his shoulder a few cars could be seen inching along. He said excitedly, "It's crazy out here, folks. The snow just keeps coming down. There's only four to five feet of visibility. So stay home and stay tuned because anything could happen."

"Obviously this bloke has never been to Woodbridge, Connecticut," said Nicole, smirking at her nail file. When she'd arrived last night she made sure that everyone understood that she was *supposed* to be skiing in the Swiss Alps with her boyfriend and some of his friends from the university, but two weekends earlier she'd wrenched her knee at Stowe and now had to sit out the rest of the season.

To Lily's mind, the weather lent the day another shot at distinction. Cristal's absent parents. Record accumulations of snow. Not to mention the five cases of beer. Maybe the power would go out, too, she thought happily.

BIT BY BIT, they advanced their claim on Cristal's house throughout the afternoon. In the back of the fridge Cristal found a bottle of Chardonnay for Nicole that she didn't think her parents would miss. Nicole made some comment about white wine in the cold weather, but eventually she took a sip and pronounced it fine. There was a Ping-Pong table in the garage, and Lily and Kyle took on Daphne and Eric, beating them four games to three. A lunch of cold cuts and cheese and an assortment of mustards was assembled from the well-stocked fridge. Cristal brought out her mother's large supply of wigs—she liked to wear them around the house, she explained with a shrug—and all the girls took turns trying them on in front of the large mirror in the entrance hall. Cristal put on a silky shoulder-length one, platinum colored. "Maybe I should cut my hair. Maybe that's what I should do." She sighed and took off the wig, throwing it on top of the others. "Then my face would look even fatter."

Courtney turned her trained eye on Cristal. "Oh, I don't know," she said, stepping behind Cristal to hold her hair back. "Actually, you've got a pretty face. You should show it more. I could trim your hair for you. I cut my sister's all the time."

Cristal smiled shyly at herself in the mirror, then turned suddenly toward the girls. "I'm so glad we all got snowed in together. I never would have believed that all of *you* would be sleeping over my house."

"Jesus, Cristal," Courtney said, "the silliest things come out of your mouth."

LILY GATHERED up as many empty cans as she could carry— the coffee table was littered with them—and brought them into the kitchen. Courtney, Eric, and Kyle were playing quarters at the kitchen table. Lily watched Courtney bounce the quarter eight times in a row into the drinking glass. After each successful shot she would slide the quarter out of the glass and with a nod designate who had to take a swig of beer. When she got on a roll, she would sometimes single out a person to pick on—usually other girls, since they made for easy victories. After a few rounds, the girl would rise unsteadily and stagger off to be sick or lie down or call an older brother to be driven home.

Lily grabbed another beer from the fridge and stood next to the table for a moment. Kyle wrapped an arm around her hip. "Come play with us. It's your turn to drink for a while."

"I am drinking," Lily said, lifting her beer. She tried to remember how many this was. She lowered her head slowly into her hand and giggled against her palm. She had no idea how many she'd had. She'd tried to pace herself, only having one beer an hour, but every time someone returned from the kitchen with a new six-pack in hand, asking "Who needs one?" she'd ripped a can from its plastic yoke, saying "I sure am thirsty today."

Occasionally she could slip into a mood where she felt she couldn't do anything wrong. There was a dangerous, dislodged feeling to this pleasure, as though she were skidding across the surface of an iceberg.

Kyle squeezed her a little closer. "We made a good team in Ping-Pong, huh?"

Lily didn't answer, just leaned into him and rested a hand on his shoulder. The weekend before last, at Cindy Alkins's house, they were sitting next to each other, playing quarters then, too, and Kyle had reached for Lily's hand under the table. He let go of it whenever his turn came, but after he was finished, he would take her hand up again and stroke his thumb across her knuckles. And he didn't make Lily drink each time he made his shot like some boys did when they liked you. He grinned up at her now, frankly meeting her eyes.

"What do we have here?" Bobby said, strolling into the room, and Lily could feel Kyle's fingers settle more firmly on her hip.

LILY CLOSED the toilet seat cover and sat back down to wait while Courtney brushed her hair. Lily figured that this constant brushing was just an excuse for Courtney to look at herself in the mirror. She shuffled through the rack of magazines jammed between the toilet and the wall: mostly *Kiplinger's Personal Finance* and *Better Homes and Gardens.* Shoved in the middle of the pile, she discovered a Victoria's Secret catalog, the pages turned back to a spread of a big-busted Spanish-looking woman wearing a sheer teddy. The woman was stretched out on a divan, her eyes lowered to the camera. Lily lifted the photo closer. "Weird," she said. "She doesn't have any nipples." She turned the page.

Courtney picked some hairs out of her brush and sighed. "Of all the people we could get snowed in with, I can't believe we got stuck with Bobby Callahan. I'm going to have to lock my door tonight. Bobby keeps trying to get me to fool around with him and he just won't take no for an answer." She lifted the brush to her head once more. "He's definitely the biggest horn dog I ever met."

"You're telling me," said Lily. "You should hear the things he's said to me."

"It just figures that I'm the one he decided to try and get," Courtney said woefully. Her head leaned and pulled against the drag of the stiff bristles in her hair.

Lily didn't answer. When had these alliances been decided? And where had she been? It wasn't that she was interested in Bobby; she just didn't like the feeling that she'd been skipped over when everyone was choosing sides. She straightened up a bit. "Well," she said, "Kyle likes me. But I think he's kind of cute." And she couldn't stop herself from adding, "I mean, don't you think so?"

"He is *so* nice," Courtney said, and Lily was pleased to see a soft dreaminess settle over her reflection. "Last year"—Courtney glanced in the mirror in the general direction of the toilet where Lily sat—"he had a crush on me and he used to call me every night. Every single night." She giggled. "My mother would be like, 'Courtney, it's that poor lovesick boy again.' He drove me crazy." She put the hairbrush down, gave herself one last approving look, and turned to face Lily. She beamed at her. "You should definitely go for him. You guys would make the cutest couple."

Lily shrugged and looked down and flipped back to the spread of the Spanish woman before replacing the magazine in the rack.

WHEN FOR the thirteenth time in a row her quarter chinked into the glass, Lily punched both fists into the air. "Since you were trying to jinx me with number thirteen, I guess this one has your name on it, Bobby Callahan."

"That's Mr. Callahan to you." Bobby reached his hand across the table and gently touched his fingertip to Lily's nose. She stayed very still. "And don't you forget it." Out of the corner of her eye, she saw Courtney look away.

"Ha! In your dreams." Lily jerked her face back and fished the quarter out.

Kyle touched her arm. "Boy, Lily, you're on—"

"You want to know what else you do in my dreams?" Bobby asked.

Kyle started again. "Jeez, Lily—"

Between snorts of laughter, Eric squeezed out, "What does she do, Bobby? What does Lily do in your dreams?"

Nicole spoke up from her perch on the kitchen stool, where she'd been watching the game. "I for one am not in the least bit interested in the inner workings of your crude little mind. I'd sooner be forced to watch the video of Nurse Keinklaupt's home birth." Everyone burst into laughter.

Nicole took a sip of her Chardonnay and smiled smugly.

"You're on some roll." Kyle was still clutching at Lily's arm.

"What is it?" Lily turned and looked at him full in the face.

"I just said how you're really on a roll. You couldn't miss if you tried."

She fingered the quarter. "Don't say that. You'll jinx me."

"Go, Lily." Daphne tapped her fingernail on the table. "You're holding up the game."

The quarter knocked the rim of the glass and bounced away. "See," Lily hissed, turning to face Kyle again, and out of her voice a viciousness rose; it coiled, swayed threateningly between them—then descended. "I told you you'd jinx me." She got up, pushing her chair back roughly, and headed upstairs to the bathroom.

It took a moment after sitting down on the toilet for the world to settle around her. She leaned back on the commode, but could not settle herself. She felt as though she had been gathered together like a bolt of fabric between two fists and then twisted taut. She stood up and shook her head in front of the mirror, shaking her hair loose from its bun. Steadying herself against the sink, she studied her face. What did Kyle see? She could feel him watching her. She could feel how his evening was being strung from one chance meeting of their eyes, one joke or touch exchanged, to the next.

She knew what he wanted—for Lily to be his girlfriend, for them to talk on the phone late at night, to sit together in the cafeteria, to walk hand in hand through the hallways of their school. He'd probably be one of those boyfriends who insists on slow dancing no matter what the song. When Lily danced, she wanted to feel wild, elated, as though at any moment she could lose control.

WHEN LILY returned to the kitchen, Eric and Daphne were wrestling on the kitchen floor. Daphne had the quarter and he was trying to grab it from her. "It's my turn. It's my turn," she kept saying. Everyone was standing around them, laughing. Daphne and Eric were laughing, too.

"I've got five dollars on her," Bobby said. "Anybody? Anybody?"

Eric rolled on top of Daphne and Lily saw him put his hand to the girl's breast as he struggled to sit up. How surprising to see Daphne's face soften. Lily wondered if a boy had ever before touched her there. Then Eric pinched her. Her hands flew up to push him away. The quarter was sent rolling across the floor. In a flash, he was off her, scrambling after it. Daphne threw a punch at his fleeing back. "Fucking asshole," she screamed. Her hand softly kneaded her breast. "You're such an asshole," she said again.

Eric resumed his seat, quarter in hand.

Bobby punched him in the arm. "Yeah, Eric. Why can't you be nice like me." He raised his eyes to Lily's. She smiled and shook her head. "How about we all kiss and make up," he said, still meeting her eyes.

They decided to make dinner. Lily offered to help Cristal, and as she chopped the carrots and tomatoes for the salad, she realized that she was exhausted and incredibly hungry.

.   .   .

AFTER THEY finished eating, Bobby insisted that they each have a glass of milk to coat their stomachs so they could keep drinking without getting sick. Lily drained her glass and lay back on the floor of the den. "Boy that hit the spot," she said. She turned to look out the window. Past the bright reflection on the glass of the overhead light, she could just make out the snow, coming down as relentlessly as before. Night had finally arrived, and they still had a long evening before them.

Eric knelt in front of the TV reading off various video titles: *The Guns of Navarone, Let's Negotiate! Ten Steps for a Better Stroke.* "You girls should watch that one."

"It's about golf, Eric," Cristal said.

Bobby reclined in the leather armchair and said, "I could use some work on my stroke. My dad said he would get me a junior membership at the club this summer."

Lily stretched her arms above her head and let out a noisy yawn. "I find golf very boring."

"Are there any decent courses around here?" Nicole asked, looking at Bobby.

"Why? Do you play?" Bobby tilted his chair upright again.

"Whenever we've lived in the States, my father's taken me to Pebble Beach. When we were in Europe, we'd go to Turnberry." She added, "It's in Scotland."

"I'm familiar with the course," Bobby said.

Lily flipped to her side and propped herself up on an elbow. She glanced behind her to see Bobby leaning forward, his hands resting on his knees. She ran her hand along the curve of her waist to lay on her hip, looked up to find Kyle watching her. She fell back and stared at the ceiling. "I'm bored."

"Well, do you guys want to watch the golf one? Should we put that one on?" Cristal addressed the room.

Daphne assured her that no one wanted to watch golf.

"So, what's your handicap," Bobby asked Nicole.

And Nicole began to answer, "That depends where—" when from the TV came, "OK baby, you want it hard?"

Lily lifted her head.

"Bingo!" Eric said, scooting back from the set. The screen was filled by a man's naked buttocks pumping forward. Instantly something released in Lily, something she hadn't realized was so close at hand, and a warmth spread down from her stomach. Rather than amazement, she felt relief at seeing the thing that had been so evasive and distracting all afternoon suddenly conjured up there on the screen.

Cristal shrieked, "Oh my God! Gross. Where did you find that?"

"Behind the others. It was the only one with no label on it."

The camera pulled back to offer a wider angle of the man's back and a pair of woman's legs clothed in black stockings and red high-heel shoes held aloft on either side of him. The woman was perched on the edge of a pool table.

"He's pounding his ball into her pocket, all right," said Bobby.

"And for a second there," Nicole said, standing up, "I thought we were actually going to have a conversation." She walked out of the room.

"Hey, Nicole," Courtney called after her, also getting up. "Where's that wine?"

"All right, you guys, turn it off." Cristal's faint command was no match for the woman's moaning.

Lily looked up to see that Daphne was also heading out of the room.

Lily sat up. "I don't see what the big deal is. It's just a dirty movie." The warmth had settled between her legs and was moving slowly out from there. She crossed her arms over her chest and eyed the screen critically.

Kyle asked her if she'd seen one of these before, but she

pretended that she didn't hear his question. She had never seen one before, or anyone doing it, for that matter. She hadn't done it herself. The only thing she knew about these movies was that they weren't made with her in mind. This wasn't the kind of sex that a girl was supposed to be interested in—this was fucking; this was vulgar—although she wasn't interested, exactly. She was spellbound. Here was the thing that all their jokes alluded to, the thing that could turn a story wild, the thing that could ruin her, if she chose the wrong time or the wrong person. Here it was right in front of her in bright, unforgiving light, to be scrutinized and criticized, to be turned on or off at whim.

"Gross," Cristal said again, sounding less convinced.

"She must be getting tired of holding her legs up like that," Lily said. Indeed, the woman had hooked a hand under one knee, and her other leg was starting to droop a bit. Yet the tempo and urgency of her moans kept steadily increasing.

"I can't watch this," Cristal blurted out, her hands over her face, and fled the room.

"She's just faking," Lily called after her. "All these women fake it, you know."

"Boy, Lily," Kyle said, sounding surprised. "I didn't know you were such an expert."

"Stop talking," Bobby said. "It's almost the climax." And he settled back in his chair as though watching porn movies were the most natural thing in the world.

"Fine," Lily said and then they were all quiet and she saw that Bobby was right—the man had begun moving faster, and the woman had settled back on her elbows, steadying herself for this final lap. Something told Lily that she should leave now. She pushed herself to her feet. "Enjoy," she called over her shoulder as she sauntered out of the room.

She found the girls seated around the kitchen table. They

stopped talking when she walked in. "I mean, it's just a stupid dirty movie," she said. "I don't see what the big deal is."

"So why are you here?" Daphne asked.

Before Lily could think of an answer, Eric hooted in the next room. "Sweet. Right on her face."

Lily held a hand up and said, "I didn't like the commentary, I guess." Daphne gave her a skeptical look.

"Splendid class of guys you hang out with," said Nicole. She looked at her watch. "Oh my God. It's almost midnight in Zurmatt. I've got to call Tom before he goes to bed." She headed out of the room, calling back to Cristal over her shoulder, "Don't worry. I'll put it on the calling card."

"I wonder why she didn't go with him," Cristal said once Nicole was out of earshot. "She'd probably be having a much better time there."

Lily stretched her fingers out on the kitchen table, examining her nails. "Maybe he didn't really invite her, after all," she ventured.

"My dad calls all over the world for his business. He wouldn't even notice a call to Switzerland." Cristal started to stand up. "I should go tell her to just call direct."

"I'm sure it's not a problem for Nicole's father either," Daphne said.

Cristal sat back down. "I can't believe those guys would rather watch a porno movie when they've got live girls right here."

"Why?" Daphne asked, her voice suddenly vehement. She leaned forward to peer into Cristal's face. "You would fool around with one of them?"

Courtney's mouth twitched up into a smile and she looked away. None of these guys would fool around with Cristal. She could have the prettiest face in the whole class and the nicest personality, too, but that still didn't make up for the fact that she was fat. Daphne knew that. Courtney knew that. And Lily knew that. So did Cristal.

"I don't know," Cristal said, looking down. "No. I guess not." She sighed. "So what do we do now?" She looked around the table, and when she didn't receive any response, her gaze wandered toward the kitchen counters. "We could make something, cookies or brownies or something . . ." Her voice trailed off. She began to twirl a strand of hair around her finger.

"I know," Courtney said. "We can cut your hair."

Daphne perked up. "That's a great idea."

Daphne's enthusiasm—its appearances were rarely constructive—made Lily interject, "I don't know. Maybe we should wait till morning. We've been drinking for a while now and . . ."

"*You've* been drinking for a while." Courtney held her hands out in front of her. "I'm steady as a rock. Go get the scissors, Cristal. It'll look great. You'll see."

CRISTAL SAT in the middle of the kitchen on a chair, her red hair hanging heavy and wet, a towel pinned around her neck. Courtney started with her bangs while Daphne combed out the rest. Lily stood in front of them, her arms crossed over her chest, and tried not to listen to the sounds coming from down the hallway. The directives of the man and the moans of the woman were interspersed with offerings from the guys, mostly Eric and Bobby, but every once in a while Kyle said something, too.

"Suck me, baby. That's right."

"Mmm. Mmmm." Eric made a sound like someone trying to talk with their mouth full.

From Kyle, "Yeah."

None of the other girls even glanced up. They seemed to have made a silent pact to pretend that they couldn't hear any of this. But Lily's mind kept supplying images to go with the noises she heard. She pictured the man's fingers grabbing the soft flesh of the woman's hips. She saw the woman tilting her head back when she'd settled onto her elbows. Her pale throat. Her dark hair brushing back and forth across the red velvet surface of the pool table. Didn't the other girls realize that the night was taking a turn, that it would veer off into more treacherous waters in this movie's wake? Cristal looked up at Lily as the other girls fussed around her. Her eyes were wide and expectant, shining with the possibility of transformation.

Courtney worked her way across Cristal's short bangs, pulling them away from her face with the wide-toothed comb and carefully snipping off a quarter inch from their ends.

"We should cut her hair short. Like mine," Daphne said. Lily raised her eyebrows. Cristal's hair—a deep red, wavy, and long, running halfway down her back—was the best thing she had going for her.

"Well, usually I just trim my sister's hair," Courtney said. "I don't know about a big style change."

"You really think I would look good with short hair?" Cristal asked.

"Definitely," Daphne said.

Courtney moved on to the side of Cristal's head, parting a small V and combing a long strand into her hand, just as Lily had seen her own hairdresser do. Courtney lifted the ends to examine them. "You definitely need a trim. You have all these split ends."

"That's why we have to cut a lot off." Daphne's hand moved down the strand until it was three inches from Cristal's head. She looked up and fixed her stare on Courtney, widening her eyes slightly. Courtney lowered the scissors and hesitated. Doubt passed briefly, almost imperceptibly across her smile, like the shadow an airplane might throw on the ground for a moment as it passed in front of the sun.

"It will look great, right, Lily?" Daphne asked. Surely Cristal heard the dishonesty in Daphne's voice. But no, there she was, glancing from Daphne to Courtney to Lily and then back again like an animal that recognizes it is being discussed but can't understand the subject is how to slaughter it.

"Deep throat, yeah," Bobby called.

Lily couldn't help laughing. "This is just great," she said, gesturing toward the den.

"OK then," Cristal said. And Courtney's hand swooped down and she was sawing through the lock. Daphne held up the chopped-off swath of hair, thrust it toward Courtney and then Lily, the ends still curling, and threw it to the ground.

Lily flinched and turned away; she found herself facing the fridge. She didn't know what to do, so she opened the refrigerator door and grabbed another beer from the waning supply.

When Lily turned back, the scissors was flying in Courtney's hands. She didn't bother with parting sections anymore. She just cut whatever piece Daphne presented. Everything was suddenly moving too quickly for Lily. She'd thought maybe Courtney would just cut a few pieces and then decide they'd had enough. Or that Cristal would stop her and ask for a mirror, that she would realize that she couldn't count on these girls' kindness. But now Lily saw that they'd passed kindness and any chance of making this right long ago. Soft pillows of red hair littered the floor.

"Now I'm going to fuck you," the man promised in the next room.

Lily watched, gulping at her beer each time her conscience threatened to articulate itself. Cristal stared up at her, and her expression was so trusting that it made Lily want to scream at her, and she had to turn away again. She walked blindly toward the den.

She paused in the doorway and closed her eyes, trying to concentrate, to think of something to do, something to say, to make things stop for a moment, to draw everyone's attention to what was happening. But the only thing she could focus on was the movie's background music: a synthesized, playful tune, moving coyly up the scale. She took another step forward and opened her eyes. The woman was pictured from the side, bent over a wooden stool. The man was behind her, getting ready to enter her.

Lily belched. She clenched her stomach and stretched her mouth open, and belched as loudly as she could. "Now I'm going to fuck you," she said in her deepest voice.

The man started with the woman, and soon her stool was rocking precariously on its forward legs.

Eric made a barking noise.

Kyle looked up at Lily. He seemed to want to meet her eye. He was saying something, but his words just passed right by her. "Are you OK?" And "You look—" Bobby was looking at her, too, his eyes wide with . . . what? Amusement? Excitement? He was waiting for her to speak.

"Are we going to do some shots or watch this stupid movie all night? Huh? What's it gonna be, Bobby boy, yes or no?"

Before Lily even had an answer, she turned around and walked back through the kitchen, the linoleum floor slippery with Cristal's hair; she walked past Daphne, who was at the same time laughing uproariously and also seemed to be trying to stop, her body twitching and twisting as though she were trying to disengage from an electrical fence; past Courtney, running her hands through the jagged, uneven clumps that were left of Cristal's beautiful red hair and still snipping haphazardly; and past Cristal, who looked delighted to see everyone having such a wild time. The guys were right behind Lily, no doubt having been commanded by Bobby to follow.

"I can't believe my dad watches pornos," Cristal shrieked, covering her face with her hands.

"Don't move," Courtney said. "You don't want me to mess up now, do you?"

Daphne's laughter rose in pitch to the higher plane of silence. She rocked back and forth, holding her belly.

Bobby spoke. "Cristal, Cristal. You look hot as a pistol."

Eric followed with "More like piss."

Lily marched through the entrance hall, yelling, "Shots! Shots! Shots! Shots!" and Nicole appeared, posed on the landing where the front stairs turned to disappear above. She had the portable phone pressed to her hip. "Do you mind? I'm on the phone to Switzerland."

"Blah. Blah. Blah. I can't hear you." Lily kept marching toward the living room, pumping her arms back and forth, stepping her knees up. Nicole held the receiver out to the room briefly and then said into it, "Do you hear this? This is what I have to deal with."

Lily stood at the bar, pouring out shots of vodka. She drank one down and passed the rest behind her. Kyle lifted his to his nose and sniffed suspiciously. "Vodka shots?" he asked.

"In Switzerland, it's all the rage," Lily assured him.

"In Switzerland," said Bobby, "if you don't drink it, then everyone gets to call you a pussy for the rest of the night."

"Who cares about Switzerland?" Kyle asked.

"Oh." Lily breathed in sharply. "I'm telling Nicole."

"Fine." Kyle drank the shot. He banged the glass down. "I could give a shit what Nicole thinks of me."

After Lily downed her second shot, she leaned up against

the bar, her back to the room. She let her head fall forward. The distance was much greater than she imagined. Her head felt as though it were traveling in slow motion through some dense substance. Like snow. How nice it would feel to be surrounded by big soft piles of snow, to crawl under that cold blanket where she could be alone with herself for a moment. She let her hands spread out on either side; her chest was almost lying on the bar. Her back lengthened slightly, arching, as she imagined someone coming up behind her and touching her. She looked over her shoulder, and Bobby was standing there. He still held that question in his face, looking at her quizzically and a little encouragingly, too: all he needed was a word from her and then he could take over.

"I want to go outside." She straightened up.

"What are you babbling about?" Eric said. "Keep pouring."

Lily didn't even put on her jacket. She waded into the yard and fell back into a drift. She looked up toward the sky, but all she could see was a screen of snow showering down at her. The flakes lodged on her lashes and made her eyes tear. As soon as the snow hit her skin, it began to melt. A warmth was spreading through her belly, down her legs, and out her arms to reach the tips of her fingers. She opened her mouth to catch the flakes on her tongue. They tasted cold and clean; she licked her lips and opened her mouth wider. She didn't know how much time had passed. At one point she saw the outside light go on, but she lay beyond the bright white circle it cast, and then Kyle appeared on the front steps. "Lily," she heard him call. "Lily. Are you all right?"

Finally she went in and managed to get upstairs without anyone seeing her. She lay down on top of one of the beds. Somewhere beneath the warmth of her drunkenness, she knew that she was very cold. She put her foot to the floor to slow her spinning and fell asleep.

OUTSIDE, the wind had picked up. Snow drifted slowly across the yard to pile up in front of the stone wall. The garden bench was barely a ripple in the landscape, and the limbs of the oak trees, cold and brittle, creaked grudgingly as the wind pulled at them. Snow blew over the hollow Lily had made, covering all traces of her.

Bobby walked unsteadily up the stairs and opened the first door he came to. The overhead light was on; someone was asleep on top of the covers. It was Lily. This was where she had disappeared to, just when they were starting to have some fun. The rest of the night had gone downhill from there. Cristal started to cry about her haircut, and nothing Daphne or Courtney could say could get her to stop. Finally Courtney had asked Bobby to go tell Cristal that she looked pretty, but when he walked into the kitchen and Cristal looked up at him, her eyes red and swollen, he said instead, "Oh, come on. Don't cry. It'll grow back. I promise." Cristal's hair would grow back eventually, but this humiliation would stay with her.

Bobby closed the bedroom door quietly behind him. He sat down on the edge of the bed. Lily's lips were a dark red and slightly parted; her breath rustled between them. He reached out one hand to touch her pant leg. It was wet and cold.

"Hey, Lily." He tapped her leg. "Wake up. You're soaking." She didn't stir. He stood up and looked back toward the door for a moment. Then he sat back down and began unbuttoning her shirt, gently laying it open. He felt the edge of her bra between two fingers: it was wet, too. He pulled her arms out of the sleeves and then slid the shirt from under her. Now her shoes. After he had them off, he unbuttoned her pants and slid them down her legs. Her panties were dragged down slightly also, and he noticed a few hairs peeking out the top. *We've got to get these wet clothes off,* he whispered and pulled her underwear back up again. He squirmed his hands underneath her back to unhook her bra. Her nipples were pointy and puckered. He brushed the back of his hand against one, running his knuckles against its cold sharp point. He got up on the bed and knelt over her; he breathed warm air on her nipple. Then he took the cold nipple into his mouth. All the while, she didn't move. Bobby's hand dropped to his crotch and he rubbed himself. He moved his mouth to her other nipple, warming that one, too.

Bobby straightened up and sat down on the edge of the mattress. He looked at her body. He had never seen a girl this undressed before. Girls would let him put his hand up their shirt or down their pants, but they always insisted on keeping their clothes on. Lily looked beautiful, so still and pale and soft. He ran his fingertips down her cheek, her throat, between her breasts, across her stomach, and down one leg to squeeze her cold toes in his hand, then up the other leg to brush across the front of her panties.

He took off his shirt and unbuttoned his pants, and without giving himself a chance to think about what he was doing, he pulled them and his underwear down to his knees. When he leaned forward to crouch over her again, he saw that Lily's eyes were open. She was looking at him. He was balanced on his feet and one hand; the other hand was between his knees, trying to push his pants down farther. She was looking at him right in the eyes, but she didn't speak. His arm and legs started trembling with the effort of holding himself up. Look away, he thought. Say something. Finally he rocked backward to his heels and yanked his pants back up, hopped off the bed, and walked out of the room.

Lily turned her face toward the floor. Her clothes, Bobby's

shirt, her bra, were strewn around the edge of the bed. When Bobby took her nipple into his mouth, she had woken, surprised to find him the source of the warmth that had brought her out of sleep. She kept her eyes shut, thinking that if she didn't respond, then he would just go away. She lay there waiting for him to get up and leave. A long moment passed and he didn't move. She kept waiting. . . . Only now it was for him to touch her again, and when at last she felt his fingertips on her cheek, down her body, leaving warm traces on each place he touched, she wasn't sure what she wanted. But when she opened her eyes, the distance between them was much less than she imagined it would be—his face hovered over hers—and she saw that what was about to happen wasn't something that could be turned on or off at whim. And once she saw that, she couldn't look away.

A NOTE ON THE TYPE

This book was set in Celeste, a typeface created in 1994 by the designer Chris Burke. He describes it as a modern, humanistic face having less contrast between thick and thin strokes than other modern types such as Bodoni, Didot, and Walbaum. Tempered by some old-style traits and with a contemporary, slightly modular letterspacing, Celeste is highly readable and especially adapted for current digital printing processes which render an increasingly exacting letterform.

Composed by Creative Graphics, Allentown, Pennsylvania
Printed and bound by Quebecor Printing, Fairfield, Pennsylvania
Designed by Robert C. Olsson